Augustus W. Clason

Seven Conventions

Augustus W. Clason

Seven Conventions

ISBN/EAN: 9783337418731

Printed in Europe, USA, Canada, Australia, Japan

Cover: Foto ©Andreas Hilbeck / pixelio.de

More available books at **www.hansebooks.com**

CONVENTIONS

BY

A. W. CLASON

NEW YORK
D. APPLETON AND COMPANY
1888

PREFACE.

What can a history of the Constitution do toward interpreting its provisions? This must be done by comparing the plain import of the words with the general tenor and object of the instrument. The instrument was written by the fingers which write this letter. Having rejected redundant and equivocal terms, I believed it to be as clear as our language would permit; excepting, nevertheless, a part of what relates to the judiciary. On that subject conflicting opinions had been maintained with so much professional acuteness, that it became necessary to select phrases which, expressing my own notions, would not alarm others nor shock their self-love; and, to the best of my recollection, this was the only part which passed without cavil. But, after all, what does it signify that men should have a written Constitution containing unequivocal provisions and limitations? The legislative lion will not be entangled in the meshes of a logical net.

The Legistature will always make the power which it wishes to exercise, unless it be so organized as to contain within itself the sufficient check. Attempts to restrain it from outrage will only render it more outrageous. The idea of binding legislators by oaths is puerile. Having sworn to exercise the powers granted according to their true intent and meaning, they will, when they desire to go further, avoid the shame if not the guilt of perjury, by swearing the true intent and meaning to be, according to their comprehension, that which suits their purpose.—*Gouverneur Morris to Timothy Pickering.*

NOTE.—On the 6th of August, 1787, the committee of five submitted the draft of a Constitution. The preamble read, "We the people of the States of New Hampshire, Massachusetts," etc., seriatim. That was accepted unanimously, and the Convention passed to and upon each other article. The number of States needed to ratify and make the Constitution a government between them was then fixed at nine. The draft when amended was sent to a committee of revision and style. As only nine States were needed to establish the Constitution, and as which nine could not be guessed, the enumeration of States was no longer possible; therefore, the "We," signifying several, and "people," being either plural or singular, the signification of the preamble first accepted and that subsequently accepted was to the minds of men at that period identical. Therefore the objection of Henry was treated as too trivial for argument. His political sagacity was awake to the possibility of the preamble being misrepresented, and dreaded the result.

CONTENTS.

SEVEN CONVENTIONS.

1776.

In the latter half of the eighteenth century two classse of colonies were connected with Great Britain—colonies by conquest, as Canada and Jamaica; colonies by settlement, those which became the United States. The political relation of the former was settled by the common consent of mankind and the usage of ages. That of the latter had not been so defined; colonies under similar conditions originated, not having before existed. The ties between Great Britain and those colonies were many and strong—a common ancestry, a common religion, a common pride of race, a common language, common political traditions, and a common share in the memories of the past, the objects of the present, and the hopes of the future. As in all political connections between a stronger and a weaker, the weaker had on some subjects suffered injustice, but none so keenly felt as to weaken a sense of union with the mother-country, or to lessen loyalty to the crown or affection for the people of England. Such a condition of things might have remained unchanged for years; it could not, after either side had determined on drawing a line which would force an issue. Neighbors with adjacent open land may be careless of metes and bounds, and indulgent to occasional trespass; but, if one begins to run a fence, the other turns to his title-deed.

Great Britain, as the stronger always will, drew a line which must force an issue. The colonies accepted the challenge. The question was simple and single. Wrong must have been wholly on one side or the other. Walpole, upon a suggestion to tax the colonies, answered, "Who does must be a bolder man than I, and less a friend to the British Constitution." The bolder man appeared, and taxation was attempted. It was not heavy; its returns for a year would not have paid the cost of an army for a week. The colonies had before contributed large free-will offerings, when the equity of such contributions was manifest to them, and were ready to do so again. But, glad to give, they denied a right to take. Upon an aggression, which involved a right of aggression, they justly thought it more wise and equally safe at once to risk all in contesting it. Submission would make a precedent for, and give color of right to future aggressions. The debate which preceded an armed solution, so far from convincing either disputant of wrong, confirmed both in their sense of right. This was inevitable, for their premises differed, and consequent reasoning from those premises developed conclusions so repugnant, that one disputant must yield unreservedly, or be made to. Those premises need to be clearly stated, not only that their irreconcilable discord may be appreciated, and the merits of the controversy correctly judged, but that the subsequent history of those colonies be understood; for the opposite theories of the relation of communities politically connected survived the contest, and men in the United States have divided into parties, one of which under various names has revived and embodied the British conception, the other retaining and embodying the colonial conception. The colonists claimed rights under the contracts of their ancestors.* After the battle of Hastings,

* So that the right of colonies (to be held commonwealths or provinces) saving honor and league with their metropoles dependeth wholly on their

William of Normandy was master of England. Part of its territory he took for the crown, part he left to the vanquished race, part he divided among his followers upon feudal tenures. The feudal system was a system of contracts: if the feudal tenant kept to the bargain, his duty was performed; if the overlord did not, and sought more than the bargain gave him, he might be justly and legally resisted. If a contest ensued, it was held legitimate war. Contract recognized as the basis of relations between freemen, resistance to an invasion of rights under contract not merely legal, but demanded by manhood, and the social elevation of women, are the legacies of the feudal system to our civilization. After the Great Charter and its numerous confirmations, all free men in England were fully recognized as entitled (subject to the law) to complete mastership of person and property. If the king, for public purposes, needed more than his own domain and the feudal tenures could supply, he asked aid of his subjects. Their right of refusal, though often evaded, was never denied. "If the king stepped over the constitutional line, they claimed the right to step over it themselves, and, that failing, promptly armed and appealed to the God of battles." Subject, then, within his kingdom to some limitations, in external matters the king was supreme. Title to land in America was in him; he dealt with it as he pleased. To have value it must be peopled; therefore he gave tracts of it to emigrants upon a tenure and rental, and charters erecting them into bodies politic and corporate, which assured them the rights and privileges of Englishmen. The transaction was wholly between the king and the emigrants; England as a nation neither supplied a penny nor furnished a man, and was then as disconnected from any right of control as Spain. The emigrants were

---

license or letters by which their sovereign authorized them to plant.—"Leviathan," p. 210.

to form communities, of which the King of England by virtue of his office was to be the king, and the relation between him and them was as easily as it was clearly defined. Whatever rights and privileges his English subjects then had, or ever afterward should have, his American subjects should also have. The bargain was one of reciprocal advantage; a consideration passed on both sides. All political systems in the United States originated from contract; political systems in Europe, with scarcely an exception, have conquest as their basis. Inattention to this difference makes all foreigners and many Americans misunderstand our political system, and not realize that much is permissible to a man as the citizen of a State, which is forbidden to him as a subject of the Constitution of the United States. Under their charters the emigrants had organized separate societies and instituted governments. Each had its elective Legislature, a judiciary, and an executive, the king. The colonies had made war upon the natives, and conquering, enslaved them; in one colony a tribe had been exterminated, and the work of extermination was progressing in all. They had coined money, issued a paper currency, pledged public credit, raised and employed armed forces on land and at sea, and like other communities had misused power to persecute dissenters from dogma, and to hang Quakers and witches.* The conclusion they drew, when forced to a logical conclusion was, that the colonies were nations, bearing the same relation to Great Britain, as Scotland had to England before the union, when their king was the same, or Hanover at that very time; and that their citizens were subjects of the king, but not subjects of his subjects. They did not

* Salem exhibited the almost solitary instance of men, protected by public functions, making a public acknowledgment that, under a delusion, they had perpetrated grave wrongs, for which they asked the forgiveness of men and the mercy of God.

press this claim, until immunity from taxation under their charters was denied; and then they could not withhold it, for, though the right of an Englishman not to be taxed without representation was their right, yet if not nations, but parts of a nation, or dependencies of a nation, and one of the three they must be, the government of Great Britain was their government, and its action, no matter how inequitable, legal.

Highly as they prized their connection with Great Britain, and strongly as their hearts yearned for the old friendly relations, they felt that, if they were to be converted into inferiors, even disastrous war, if it aggravated servitude, must leave them self-respect. The British argument is nowhere so clearly stated or so closely reasoned as in the "Taxation no Tyranny." The premises of that very able paper are: Land in the colonies, in the view of political law, is the territory of England, and the colonists are units of the English nation; the Parliament is their Parliament, in which they are virtually represented as the greater number of Englishmen who have no votes are virtually represented; consequently that Parliament, as the delegated sovereignty of the nation, supreme in all things, may legally if not equitably alter or repeal any charter, and impose any law or duty. England, from the nature of things the stronger element in the nation, both in numbers and wealth, is necessarily the preponderant portion, and as such ought to command, while the colonies, as the minority of the nation, ought to obey. If the colonists have the rights and privileges of Englishmen, they must be subject to the obligations of Englishmen. The issue, nation or nations, could not be more distinctly presented. If the premises were true, the conclusion was legitimate and true, and the Americans must have been, as they seemed to Johnson and to three fourths of his countrymen, insubordinate from avarice, or malignant from obstinacy. But the premises were not true, because not based upon the genesis of the colonies, nor of the word nation. Nation has but one meaning, and can have no other. It is the mark by which mankind have agreed to express the fact that a certain number of human beings, inhabiting a defined territory, have coalesced by consent, or been compacted by conquest, into a general copartnership, having feelings for each other very different from those they entertain toward the rest of mankind, extending among themselves sympathy, and distributing and regulating selfishness.* In a nation there can be but one sovereignty, Force; and one standard of right and wrong, its Will; therefore Johnson properly deduced his conclusion that, if the colonists were units of a nation, resistance to the act of the sovereign was a violation of the social order. He saw clearly that "in sovereignty there are no gradations; there must be in every society some power from which there is no appeal, which admits no restrictions, which pervades the whole mass of the community, regulates and adjusts all subordination, enacts laws and repeals them, erects or annuls judicatures, extends or controls privileges, exempt itself from question or control, and bounded only by physical necessity. By this power, wherever it subsists, all legislation is animated and controlled; from this all legal rights are emanations which, whether equitably or not, may be legally recalled. It is not infallible, for it may do wrong; but it is irresistible, for it can only be resisted by rebellion, by an act which makes it questionable what shall thenceforward be the supreme power." This truth, familiar to antiquity, apparent to all who think, was so far from being controverted by the colonists that they made it the basis of all their reason-

* "Nation" is often used as a convenient abbreviation in a non-technical sense, they who use and they who hear conscious of the impropriety. So we say habitually the sun rises and sets, not thereby denying the Copernican theory.

ing and action. His own exposition of sovereignty should have shown to Johnson that men not under one single and exclusive government can not be the units of a nation. That objection pressed him so sharply that he could only find escape from it by the assumption that a colony in America and a county in England were politically identical. As Great Britain really, though incidentally, through the king, exercised some important functions of government affecting the colonies, he may have confounded government with sovereignty, as more acute minds have before and since, honestly or dishonestly. The colonists, however, were familiar with the distinction between original and derivative power, and knew that sovereignty makes and unmakes governments. To an American confusion on the subject ought to be impossible, for he knows that in thirteen communities governments were in full and complete operation while the sovereignty in each was debating and deciding upon a new distribution of the functions of government between two agencies, delegating power after it had decided. In the lifetime of Johnson's father the army which had defeated Charles I was sovereign in England. It offered terms to the king, and, agreement failing, struck off his head. It turned Parliament out-of-doors, it set up Oliver Cromwell, it pulled down Richard Cromwell, not representing the feelings or opinions of one fourth of Englishmen, it ruled them as absolutely as the Conqueror William, nor did it cease to be the sovereign until weakened by dissension it ceased to be the force. Government within a nation is the functionary of the society to maintain peace and order among its different elements and to adjust the relations between the stronger and the weaker. It continues unchanged so long as the proportion of strength and weakness remains unchanged. It properly, because equitably, changes, as the proportion of strength and weakness changes. The right of future management is the same as the right of original management; the reason for both, the welfare of the society.* A government of all of them in communities politically connected, is their functionary to maintain the original terms of union between equals; the shifting of strength is not a shifting of right; disputes between them are to be decided, if justly, by the law of contract, not by that of force, either expressed in numbers or by armies.† Great Britain, ignorant or careless of the only rule under which connected communities can abide together in peace, assumed mastership. If the practical wisdom of her great war minister, or the genius of her great philosophical statesman, could have saved her from (what now all admit) a silly scheme of discord, they were not wanting. Chatham not merely justified the colonies in resistance to taxation, but in armed resistance. He reminded the Lords that what is known as the British Constitution is certain accepted principles of political rights evolved in the growth of the nation; that representation inseparable from taxation was one of those rights, and that the colonists had been guaranteed its protection. He warned them that contempt of constitutional restraint, unjust to America in the present, must work harm to Great Britain in the future, and, prescient of that future, pointed to France and Spain, eagerly watching the maturity of

---

* The distinction between the nobility and the commons was originally a real one—that is, it was grounded upon a real superiority, physical or moral. But every successive generation tended to make it more and more imaginary, till, at the moment of the final struggle between the two orders, it had no real existence at all. The commons then had become as well qualified as the nobles, both physically and morally, to conduct the affairs of peace and war. —*Arnold*, Preface to "Thucydides."

† The claim in the "Leviathan" that a commonwealth can alienate its sovereignty, and that any government it institutes is an entity distinct from and master of it, not its agent, was supposed buried with the *jure divino*. It has been revived in the United States by such respectable authority as to merit a rehearing.

error for the opportunity of war. Burke declined to discuss a right of taxation. Evidently, to his mind, if it did not exist, there was an end of controversy; if its existence was so doubtful that men might honestly differ, Englishmen had no right to force their new conclusions upon Americans; and if it did exist, its exercise would be inexpedient, unwise, and unjust, considering the relations up to that period subsisting. "Such is my opinion of the absolute necessity of keeping up the concord of this empire by a unity of spirit, though in a diversity of operations, that, if I were sure that the colonists had, on leaving this country, sealed a regular contract of servitude, that they had solemnly abjured all rights of citizens, that they had made a vow to renounce all ideas of liberty for them and their posterity to all generations; yet I should hold myself obliged to conform to the temper I found universally prevalent in my own day, and to govern two millions of men, impatient of servitude, upon the principles of freedom. I am not determining a point of law, I am restoring tranquillity; and the general character and situation of a people must determine what sort of a government is fitted for them. That point nothing else can or ought to determine. In the character of the Americans a love of freedom is the predominating feature, which marks and distinguishes the whole; and, as an ardent is always a jealous affection, your colonies become suspicious, restive, and untractable, whenever they see the least attempt to wrest from them by force, or shuffle from them by chicane, what they think the only advantage worth living for. This fierce spirit of liberty is stronger in the English colonies, probably, than in any other people of the earth, for the colonists emigrated from you when this part of your character was most predominant, and they took the bias and direction the moment they parted from your hands. They are therefore not only devoted to liberty, but to liberty according to

English ideas and upon English principles. Abstract liberty, like other mere abstractions, is not to be found. Libberty inheres in some sensible object, and every nation has formed to itself some favorite point, which, by way of eminence, becomes the criterion of their happiness. It happened that the great contests for freedom in this country were from the earliest times chiefly upon the question of taxing. Most of the contests in the ancient commonwealths turned primarily on the right of election of magistrates, or on the balance among the several orders in the state. The question of money was not with them so immediate. But in England it was otherwise; on this point the ablest pens and most eloquent tongues have been exercised, the greatest spirits have acted and suffered. In order to give the fullest satisfaction concerning the importance of this point, it was not only necessary for those who in argument defended the excellence of the English Constitution to insist on this privilege of granting money as a dry point of fact, and to prove that the right had been acknowledged in ancient parchments, and blind usages, to reside in a certain body called a House of Commons; they went much further: they attempted to prove, and they succeeded, that in theory it ought to be so, from the particular nature of a House of Commons as the immediate representative of the people, whether the old records had delivered this oracle or not. They took infinite pains to inculcate, as a fundamental principle, that in all monarchies the people must in effect, themselves, mediately or immediately, possess the power of granting their own money, or no shadow of liberty could subsist. The colonies draw from you, as with their life-blood, these ideas and principles. Their love of liberty, as with you, is fixed and attached on this specific point of taxing. Liberty might be safe, or be endangered, in twenty other particulars, without their being much pleased or alarmed. Here they felt its pulse, and as they found that beat, they thought themselves sick or sound. I do not say whether they were right or wrong in applying your general arguments to their own case. It is not easy, indeed, to make a monopoly of theorems and corollaries. The fact is, that they did thus apply your general arguments, and your mode of governing them, whether through lenity or indolence, through wisdom or mistake, confirms them in the imagination that they, as well as you, have an interest in those common principles." To the assertion that a power of granting vested in the assemblies of the colonies would dissolve the unity of the empire, he answered: "Perhaps I am mistaken in my idea of an empire as distinguished from a single state or kingdom. An empire is an aggregate of many states under one common head, whether that head be a monarch or a presiding republic. I do not know what this unity means, nor has it ever been heard of, that I know, in the constitutional policy of this country. The very idea of subordination of parts excludes the notion of simple and undivided unity. England is the head, but she is not the head and the members too. My hold on the colonies is in the close affection which grows from common names, from kindred blood, from similar privileges, and equal protection. These are the ties which, though light as air, are as strong as links of iron. Let the colonies always keep the idea of their civil rights associated with your government, and they will cling and grapple to you, and no force under heaven will be of power to tear them from their allegiance. But let it be understood that your government may be one thing, and their privileges another, that these two things may exist without any mutual relation, the cement is gone, the cohesion is loosened, and everything hastens to decay and dissolution. . . . Reconciliation," urged Burke, "can hardly be expected, if it must depend upon the juridical determination of perplexing questions, or on the precise marking of the shadowy boundaries of a complex government; but it is certain, upon a return to that path of peace which Great Britain and the colonies have for so many years trod together, with security, advantage, and honor." The resolutions of Burke, framed upon the spirit of his speech, were negatived by 270 to 78, and the preponderance of opinion was even greater in the nation than in the House. In the colonies the position was almost exactly reversed: three fourths held Great Britain in the wrong, one fourth in the right, technically, if ungenerously. That the ministry, the king, or the English people, were consciously unjust, is far from the truth. The causes of their misconception are obvious. After continuous civil contests, accompanied by two civil wars, much of the power of the crown had passed to the nation, but the old form was preserved, and all service, civil or military, is still her Majesty's. Whatever right of government over the colonies had been vested in the king, passed as had his other powers, undoubtedly with their full assent; but the obligation of the contract between him and them was the same, shared or retained. No more could pass than he possessed; king, lords, and commons had no larger right of rule than the king formerly. The power Great Britain saw, for power is easily seen; the limitation was overlooked, for limitation, except by those it protects, is easily overlooked. The taxation of Americans by Parliament seemed an ordinary and natural exercise of power to men whom it continuously taxed. The recognition of its right of complete authority, by all subjects except one portion, made the denial of such authority by that portion apparently factious. Even to entertain the idea of the contention of the colonies, an Englishman had to get out of his usual habit of thought. Had the question not become a party question, men might possibly have appreciated distinctions and reasoned without bias; but, with party spirit enlisted, taxation had to be compelled, that opponents might be confuted. Bitterness against the colonists, absent from the Taxation no Tyranny, is intense against their English advocates.

"Far be it from an Englishman to thirst for the blood of his fellow-subjects. Those who most deserve our resentment are unhappily at a less distance. The Americans, when the Stamp Act was first proposed, disliked it undoubtedly, as every nation dislikes an impost, but they had no thought of resisting it till they were encouraged and incited by European intelligence from men whom they thought their friends, but who were friends only to themselves. On the original contrivers of mischief let an insulted nation pour out its vengeance. With whatever design they have inflamed this pernicious contest, they are themselves equally detestable. If they wish the success of the colonies, they are traitors to this country; if they wish their defeat, they are traitors at once to America and to England. To them, and to them only, must be imputed the interruption of commerce and the miseries of war, the sorrow of those that shall be ruined, and the blood of those that shall fall." No words ever painted more vividly the fate of him who, appreciating its danger, opposes some darling scheme of his people. For him the future is black; with failure he is a mourner, with success a victim. Another and perhaps the leading cause for the misjudgment of Great Britain was the misapplication of the principle of majorities and minorities. That upon a controverted point of constitutional rights, less than three millions should not defer to eight millions seemed the unfairness of arrogance. The principle so consonant to reason and so salutary when interests are identical, or consequences will be equally shared, becomes a pure despotism when they are not. To crown all, the very liberality and loyalty of the colonies told against them. They had "given to satiety," and were ready to give again. If they were willing to part with their money, was not collision upon a mode of transfer not merely the unreason but the wickedness of pride?

That Great Britain was in the wrong is undeniable, but no people ever had greater excuse for being in the wrong, and none with an object of desire to compass has ever been honest enough to cast the first stone at her. War came, of course; between communities of equal civilization and spirit the result is a question of resources. "The last louis d'or wins." The colonies would have been subjugated, had not France very early secretly encouraged and aided them, soon to become an open ally. Then the disparity of force shifted,* and Great Britain was forced to recognize each State as the independent community which the Declaration of Independence had announced it as such to the world. The fate of that famous paper is singular. For more than fifty years it has been assumed by many to mean what it does not say, and not to mean what it does say; though there never has been a collection of words of which the intention is more palpable or its expression more exact. Its propositions are four: that men are created free and equal, entitled to life, liberty, and the pursuit of happiness; that to secure those rights they form societies and institute governments; that just governments are founded on the consent of the governed; that a society has the right to alter, or to unmake, and to make a new government. These it terms self-evident truths. If self-evident, they can not be novelties; if truths, they must be true for all time and under all circumstances. Their truth may be tested at once by taking their converse, and drawing conclusions from it.

* On August 31, 1781, Count de Grasse entered Chesapeake Bay with twenty-eight ships-of-the-line, six frigates, and three thousand soldiers, the equivalent of thirty-five thousand men, which, in the exhausted state of the principals, brought the contest to an end.

Then their self-evidence will result from the nature of the human mind. That men in a state of nature are free and equal, and may do as they like, and take what they please, if they can, few would venture to deny. A great writer,* two centuries since, not only asserted that fact, but proved it with the rigor of mathematical demonstration. But the freedom and equality of all, is equivalent to the freedom and equality of none; the plus one to each, is minus the infinity of plus ones to the rest. Such is the condition of beasts. Men, having reason and speech, learned and communicated to each other the necessity of society. They gave nothing in forming it, they exchanged mutual irresponsibility for mutual responsibilities; each put into a common fund the freedom and equality he could not maintain for himself, and got in return as much as society could maintain for him. Whether the family was the original of society or not, agreement in one of its forms, consent or assent, must have been the basis of it. The idea of rights could not enter the mind until a society had been formed, nor kept out of it afterward. Only society could say, as it did at once, *Propriamque dicabo.* Experience, which had led to the formation of society, taught men that its collective force must be placed somewhere to compel the observance of the conditions of its being. Then, by consent or assent, government was instituted. One characteristic has marked every society; none have recognized the right of a man, by reason of a common humanity, to become a member of it; all have recognized that right in the progeny of members, and in all, when the consent of the governed is spoken of; the "governed" have been

* Hobbes, contending that a monarchy, an aristocracy, or a democracy, must equally and necessarily be despotic, and that a mixed government, no matter in what proportions compounded of the three, must after constant dissensions and civil war be resolved into one of the simple forms, reiterates the original freedom and equality of man to superfluity.

understood to be those entitled to political power; its members by descent or admission. What the Declaration did not say is as apparent as what it did say. It did not say that men born in a social state are entitled to the irresponsibility of the savage state. It is not an evangel of anarchy.* It did not say that government must be founded on the consent of the governed, for the facts of history were opposed; and many governments existed, founded on conquest. It did not moot questions of forms of government or functions of government; it said to what kind "just" was applicable. It did not, as supposed by those who do not weigh words, assert a right of revolution. Revolution makes a right, it does not start with one; it is not the alteration of a government by a society, it is the alteration by part of a society irregularly and forcibly, and by such a part as is the stronger, whether the few or the many. When the interests of parts of a society have become totally divergent, and passions thereby have passed beyond its control, its basis no longer exists, its members have reverted to the savage state, in which force must settle some new conditions under which peace and order may again be possible. The colonies could not have asserted a right of revolution against Great Britain without stultifying themselves, and admitting what they had so long and so persistently denied; for revolution proclaims that existing rights ought no longer to exist; while they were contending that existing rights, between contracting men and connected communities, ought to exist, as they had existed. In cases of contract between men, or connection between communities—for only by contract, express or implied, can communities have been peaceably connected—"the force of

* Baldly stated, reason revolts at the proposition, but as the higher law it was welcomed by many who may have to meet it under some other name.

words being too weak to hold men to their covenants, there are in human nature but two imaginable helps to it: a fear of the consequences of breaking their word, or a glory and pride in appearing not to need to break it; the latter a generosity too rarely found, to be presumed on, especially in the pursuers of wealth, command, or sensual pleasure, which are the greater part of mankind. Therefore, unless the parties to a question covenant mutually to stand to the sentence of an arbitrator, they are as far from peace as ever; and, seeing that every man is presumed to do all things to his own benefit, no man is fit to be an arbitrator in his own cause; and if he were never so fit, yet equity allowing each party equal benefit, if one is admitted to judge, the other is also, and so the controversy which is the cause of war remains" Unless this reasoning can be controverted, the mind can only conceive one solution of peace where no arbitrator has been chosen: that the contract be considered canceled. War may indeed find another, but if it ascertains which of the disputants is the stronger, it can not establish which of them was in the right. The colonists did not say that their fourth proposition was self-evident to force, but to reason, and they applied it to the situation, announcing to the world that whatever the nature of the political connection between them and Great Britain, that power had severed it by attempting to exercise an unwarrantable jurisdiction over them. They could not do otherwise, for on the connection was based that claim of jurisdiction.

Following the precept and example of England in 1688, they declared that the king had forfeited his right to reign over them, for aiding and abetting his other subjects in an invasion of their liberties. The assent of a colony to an announcement that the connection with Great Britain was dissolved, and that the king had ceased to reign, was its declaration of independence.* In 1787, when twelve of the States met in a convention to make a system different from that existing, the mass of men in each State believed in its nationality, on which they had argued so long, and for which they had fought so hard and suffered so much. To them the truths of the Declaration were still self-evident. Their conviction that an unlimited government must end in imbecility or bloodshed, had been strengthened by the disasters which had followed the attempt by Great Britain to overpass limitation, and they held that system of government the best which permitted the widest liberty, personal, social, and political, compatible with order. There was, however, in each State a minority, far from insignificant in number, and comprising men of rare ability, which did not have faith in the governmental practicability of the majority opinions, but they could not formulate their ideas into any plan which might be submitted to the Convention.† The Constitution which that Convention elaborated through many compromises, and submitted to the decision of the people of each State in their sovereign character, is very simple and equitable, if made by nations for nations; uselessly complex and inequitable, if made by a nation for a nation. The improvements upon the federal systems of antiquity, and upon the Articles of Confederation, were marked. The principal are: The right of rule limited in the Union by

* New York did not vote for the Declaration. Her convention assented *some days later.*

† Mason wrote from the Convention: "When I first came here (where on pecuniary considerations I would not serve for a thousand pounds a day), judging from casual conversations with gentlemen from the different States, I was very apprehensive that, soured and disgusted with the unexpected evils we had experienced from the democratical principles of our government, we should be apt to run into the opposite extreme, of which I think there is still some danger, though I have the pleasure to find in the convention some men of fine republican principles."

an enumeration of specific objects; in a State, by an exclusion of specific objects; the action of Federal powers similar to the action of such powers in a nation; Federal suffrage in each State such as the State chooses for itself; the regulation of commerce, interstate and international; revenue from its own resources of taxation; the decision of war and peace; a mode of amendment; the addition of new States; the right to prescribe the conditions under which a State may confer citizenship; a judiciary for questions in law and equity arising under the Constitution; citizenship in one State entitled to the rights and privileges of citizenship in other States; and the political influence of a State in the conduct of common interests, growing with its growth, and diminishing with its decline, through representation in one branch of a Legislature proportioned to population, equity to numbers giving them due weight; and equity to States, confining a State to an equal voice in the other branch of the Legislature. The plan, on paper, was as near perfection as any federal government (the best of all) can be; none ever united so much strength with so much liberty. But *Quis custodiet?* was instantly asked by those whose belief in a limited government was not a speculation, but a religion. A minority of States with a majority of population found a check in the instrument, a majority of States with a minority of population equally found a check; but where was the check to a majority of States, with a majority of population? If each State remained jealous of its nationality and respecting the nationality of the others, or if the voter held federal suffrage a trust, not a property to subserve desire, there would be no danger, but neither could be expected of human nature. Still less could it be expected of human nature that a man, no matter how tenacious of a limited government, would fight his own State to secure it to another State. The objection would have prevented the establishment of the

Constitution, had not its advocates offered to put in it explicitly by amendment (as it was once thought was done) the doctrine of the Declaration of Independence which they insisted was already there by implication. Both advocates and opponents understood the offer to mean that limitation had the same right to be, as government to be, deriving title from the same source, expressed in the same instrument, and vested with equal right of self-defense. As none could deny that authority, from the nature of man, is constantly impinging on liberty, the issue between the advocates and opponents of ratification was, whether the equal rights of limitation and authority were to be found in the paper as it read; the advocates insisting that they were, and the opponents contending that liberty ought not to depend upon inference, but should be guarded by language not susceptible of doubt, nor permitting misinterpretations. If a limited government can exist (still a problem), it can only exist by men being willing to put all at hazard to maintain limitation.* If it is not worth that price, they will neither keep it, nor deserve it. Again and again the kings of England endeavored to escape from the restrictions of Magna Charta; as often, they were confronted by men eager to die for it, and they prudently desisted and reconfirmed it. Had not there been many in England, in all periods of its history, who held limitation as sacred as government, Englishmen would not be what they now are, nor England what it is.

* A small piece of string is a very insignificant matter, but, if the pudding-bag is not tied with one, the mixture within becomes a mass. Limitation is to government what the string is to the bag—it helps by hindering.

THE FEDERAL CONVENTION.

On the 25th of May, 1787, a convention met at Philadelphia, and proceeded to consider the subject for which it had assembled. At that period and long after, States, independent communities, masters of themselves, entitled to withdraw the delegation of their sovereignty from the Union then existing, were supposed to be there represented. The constant assertion of such a right in the Convention, and its action in providing that nine States might make a Union separate from the other four, would seem to have embodied the belief then, and to have justified it later. Respect for a contrary opinion, now dominant, requires that the reasoning which has corrected the earlier misconception of the political rights of communities, should be set forth in its own language; the subtilty of the argument might escape in any attempt to condense it:

"Our States have neither more nor less power than that reserved to them in the Union by the Constitution, no one of them having ever been a State out of the Union. The original ones passed into the Union even before they cast off their British colonial dependence. The new ones came into the Union from a condition of dependence, except Texas, and even Texas in its temporary independence was never designated a State. The new ones only took the designation of State on coming into the Union, while the name was first adopted by the old ones by and in the Declaration of Independence. The 'United Colonies' were declared to be free and independent States, but even then the object plainly was not to declare their independence of one another or of the Union, but directly the contrary, as their mutual pledge and their mutual action before, at the time, and afterward abundantly show. The express plighting of faith by each and all of the original thirteen in the Articles of Confederation, two years later, that the Union shall be perpetual, is most conclusive. The States have their status in the Union, and they have no other legal status. Originally some dependent colonies made the Union, and in turn the Union threw off their dependence for them and made them States, such as they are. Not one of them had a State Constitution independent of the Union."

The assertion, in defiance of their denial, maintained by war, that the colonies were, as Great Britain claimed them to be, dependencies, is a fitting preface to as much misstatement of history as was ever compressed into so few lines. In 1775 the colonies proclaimed to the world that they had not raised armies with the ambitious design of separating from Great Britain and establishing independent States, but to repel aggressions on their rights. In January, 1776, New Hampshire had its self-constituted system; in March, South Carolina; in June, Virginia—the governments of each in full and harmonious action. In July the colonies announced to the world that they were free and independent States. The cause is too patent for misconception or misstatement, and the men of 1776 understood too well what they meant, and how to express their meaning, for their words or actions to need or to admit of interpretation. After and not till after the Declaration did they attempt to organize a Union, and their delegates were instructed to do the one and to attempt the other. On the 1st of March, 1781, a Union for the first time existed; its Congress met the next day. A union is a corporation, of which communities are the corporators; a community is a

corporation, of which human beings are the corporators. The second of the Articles of Confederation, through the acceptance of which only a Union existed, is explicit: "Every State retains its sovereignty, freedom, and independence, and every power, jurisdiction, and right which is not by this Confederation expressly delegated to the United States in Congress assembled." Then there must have been States mutually recognized as sovereign, and independent of each other; whence, else, that portion of jurisdiction, right, and power contributed to a common fund? Two years after a Union had been in full action, Great Britain was required to and did acknowledge, not a Union, but the independence of each State separately, name by name, in the treaty of peace. The "perpetual Union" was dissolved in a few years by the exercise of such sovereignty as made it. A new Union ("perpetual" dropped) was established by an exercise of the sovereignty of the States separately, its Constitution carefully disclaiming any right in any State or number of States over another, or any duty not self-imposed, of one State to another. Rhode Island and North Carolina were out of the existing Union when its Constitution was the government of eleven States. What was their status? New York and another State did not ratify until a new Union existed; what was their status before ratification? Finally, what was the status of those communities which had proclaimed themselves States, before the Articles of Confederation made a Union? To Great Britain they were rebel colonies; what were they to each other? If more facts than these are necessary to demonstrate the absurdity of a Union making States, instead of States making a Union, the debates in the Federal Convention will supply them. To appreciate those debates, the relative strength of the States must be kept in mind. Virginia was the most populous by one third, but half the population was negro slaves; Massachusetts was the most powerful, having nearly four hundred thousand inhabitants, almost exclusively white. Pennsylvania followed her closely in numbers, wealth, and the characteristics of race. The three contained forty-two ninetieths of the population of the United States. So far in every Congress they each had but a single vote, and were naturally and reasonably desirous of greater weight in a new system, if one could be obtained, or in some modification of that existing, which would effect their object. There was no settled indisposition on the part of the smaller States to concede to them an increase of influence. How, and how much, were cardinal points which had to be settled before the machinery of a government could gain close attention?

Business was opened by the submission of "the Virginia plan," which was made the basis of debate; those of Pinckney, more coincident with that adopted than any other, of Hamilton, and of Patterson, need not be detailed. They were not without influence upon individuals and committees, for it is apparent that in this, as in all other conventions and legislative bodies, much of the heaviest work was done by members who made few speeches, and in committees which have left no record of their labors but their reports.

VIRGINIA PLAN.

1. *Resolved*, That the Articles of Confederation ought to be so corrected and enlarged as to accomplish the objects proposed by their institution, namely, common defense, security of liberty, and general welfare.

2. *Resolved*, Therefore, that the rights of suffrage in the national Legislature ought to be proportioned to the quotas of contribution, or to the number of free inhabitants, according as the one or the other rule may seem best in different cases.

3. *Resolved*, That the national Legislature ought to consist of two branches.

4. *Resolved*, That the members of the first branch of the national

Legislature ought to be elected by the people of the several States every —— for the term of ——, to be of the age of —— years at least; to receive liberal stipends by which they may be compensated for the devotion of their time to the public service, to be ineligible to any office established by a particular State or under the authority of the United States except those peculiarly belonging to the functions of the first branch during the term of service and for the space of —— after its expiration; to be incapable of re-election for the space of —— after the expiration of their term of service, and to be subject to recall.

5. *Resolved*, That the members of the second branch of the national Legislature ought to be elected by those of the first out of a proper number of persons nominated by the individual Legislatures; to be of the age of —— years, at least to hold their offices for a term sufficient to insure their independency, to receive liberal stipends, by which they may be compensated for the devotion of their time to the public service; and to be ineligible to any office established by a particular State, or under the authority of the United States except those peculiarly belonging to the functions of the second branch during the term of service and for the space of —— after the expiration thereof.

6. *Resolved*, That each branch ought to possess the right of originating acts; that the national Legislature ought to be empowered to enjoy the legislative rights vested in Congress by the Confederation, and, moreover, to legislate in all cases to which the separate States are incompetent, or in which the harmony of the United States may be interrupted by the exercises of individual legislation; to negative all laws passed by the several States contravening in the opinion of the national Legislature the Articles of Union, or any treaty subsisting under the authority of the Union; and to call forth the force of the Union against any member of the Union failing to fulfill its duty under the articles thereof.

7. *Resolved*, That a national Executive be instituted, to be chosen by the national Legislature for the term of ——; to receive punctually at stated times a fixed compensation for the services rendered, in which no increase or diminution shall be made so as to affect the magistracy existing at the time of increase or diminution, and to be ineligible a second time; and, that, besides a general authority to execute the national, it ought to enjoy the executive rights vested in Congress by the Confederation.

8. *Resolved*, That the Executive and a convenient number of the

national judiciary ought to compose a council of revision, with authority to examine every act of the national Legislature before it shall operate and every act of a particular Legislature before a negative thereon shall be final; and that the dissent of the said council shall amount to a rejection unless the act of the national Legislature shall be again passed, or that of a particular Legislature be again negatived by —— of the members of each branch.

9. *Resolved*, That a national judiciary be established; to consist of one or more supreme tribunals; to be chosen by the national Legislature; to hold their offices during good behavior; to receive punctually at stated times fixed compensation for their services, in which no increase or diminution shall be made so as to affect the persons actually in office at the time of such increase or diminution. That the jurisdiction of the inferior tribunal shall be to hear and determine in the first instance and of the superior tribunal to hear and determine in the *dernier ressort* all piracies and felonies on the high-seas, captures from an enemy, cases in which foreigners or citizens of other States applying to such jurisdiction may be interested, or which respect the collection of the national revenue, impeachments of any national officers, and questions which may involve the national peace and harmony.

10. *Resolved*, That provision ought to be made for the admission of States lawfully arising within the limits of the United States, whether from a voluntary junction of territory, or otherwise, with the consent of a number of voices in the national Legislature less than the whole.

11. *Resolved*, That a republican government and the territory of each State except in the instance of a voluntary junction of government and territory ought to be guaranteed by the United States to each State.

12. *Resolved*, That provision ought to be made for the continuance of Congress and their authorities and privileges until a given day after the reform of the Articles of Union shall be adopted, and for the completion of all their engagements.

13. *Resolved*, That provision ought to be made for the amendment of the Articles of Union whenever it shall seem necessary; and that the assent of the national Legislature ought not to be required thereto.

14. *Resolved*, That the legislative, executive, and judiciary powers, within the several States, ought to be bound by oath to support the Articles of Union.

15. *Resolved*, That the amendments which shall be offered to the Confederation by the Convention ought, at a proper time or times after the approbation of Congress, to be submitted to an assembly or assemblies of representatives recommended by the several Legislatures to be expressly chosen by the people to consider and decide thereon.

No sooner were the Virginia resolutions before the House, than Randolph, who had introduced them, moved that the consideration of the first be postponed, and that in its place three new propositions be debated:

1. That a Union of States, merely federal, will not accomplish the objects proposed by the Articles of Confederation, namely, common defense, security of liberty, and general welfare.

2. That no treaty, or treaties, among the whole or part of the States as individual sovereignties, would be sufficient.

3. That a national Government ought to be established, consisting of a supreme Legislature, executive, and judiciary.

Gouverneur Morris (Pennsylvania), who had suggested the supersedure of the first resolution of the Virginia plan by the new propositions, recalled to the Convention the distinction between a federal and a national supreme government: the former being a mere compact, resting on the good faith of the parties; the latter having a complete and compulsive operation. The Convention refused to consider the first two, and adopted the latter. Then, turning to the Virginia plan, it postponed the second resolution, and carried the third, and so much of the fourth as made a popular vote applicable to the elections for the first branch of a contemplated Legislature. Upon the fifth resolution the smaller Northern States stopped. If not unwilling to give the larger States additional power, because additional power was equitable, when the larger States sought at once to be States and the Union, enabled to exact and to refuse good faith, they saw clearly the intended dominion, a domination of the most offensive kind, of

State over State. Therefore, they said, States in a Union is an idea not only familiar, but intelligible. States in a nation, States in a State, is a contradiction in terms. You want a nation; we do not, but we will gratify you. Open the map, divide the territory into thirteen districts as equal as possible, then your scheme is feasible and acceptable, for a nation has counties, a Union has States. Choose. To Wilson, who was perpetually urging, "We come here to make a government for men, not for imaginary beings—States," they said, "Why, then, should there be a Pennsylvania?" To Madison and Randolph, "A Virginia would be an anomaly." To King and Gorham, "The Commonwealth of Massachusetts will be an *imperium in imperio.*" Either their proposition was too fair to be gainsaid, or their reasoning too just to be refuted, for the word "national," as characterizing the proposed system, was dropped without debate and with universal assent, and is nowhere to be found in the finished work of the Convention. Hamilton had indirectly, though undesignedly, contributed to a result so opposite to his views. His intellect was too clear not to see that a Union and a nation were things as opposite as black and white. He was too fearless to conceal his convictions, and therefore proposed the abolition of States.

"By an abolition of the States, he meant that no boundary could be drawn between the national and the State Legislatures; that the former must, therefore, have indefinite authority. If it were limited at all, the rivalship of the States must gradually subvert it. Even as corporations, the extent of some of them, as Virginia, Massachusetts, etc., would be formidable. As States, he thought they ought to be abolished." Wilson did not wish that fate for Pennsylvania, nor King for Massachusetts, nor Madison for Virginia, nor Butler for South Carolina; and, brought squarely up to decide whether they would retain

States and maintain the federal principle, or extinguish the States, and essay the national principle, their choice was made at once. Why they who were willing to form units of a nation as men, if the States were fused into a mass, and the mass divided into counties, were unwilling to form a Union, statehood retained, except upon a federal basis, resulted from their minds being as incapable of conceiving divided sovereignty as of a thing in two places at once. Each State, at that time, had all the characteristics of a nation—interests, habits, an association of ideas, belief of, and pride in, its nationality, and a self-constituted political system, adjusting rights among its people, and relations with the other States. Fusion into a nation had its advantages and disadvantages; confederation had its advantages and disadvantages, but the plan submitted appeared to distribute the advantages both of a nation and of a Union to some States, and the disadvantages of both to the others, to give to some all the rights of conquest and to deny to the others the right of legal resistance. In a Union the minority of a State not only does not count for, but counts against, the opinion it holds. If a State has a million of voters, an excess of five hundred on one side carries the political power of a million, and will balance an excess of five hundred thousand in another million. That is the disadvantage of the federal plan, which the smaller States were willing to risk, if the benefit of the federal plan accompanied it, the right of judgment upon a breach of faith, and of action upon the judgment, or they would be satisfied with the absorption of statehood, because then man would count for man, and, if an issue passed from words to blows, could fight as he thought.

Their resolve was expressed in language not to be misunderstood. Ellsworth was sure "that, to the eastward, Massachusetts was the only State that would listen to a proposition for excluding the States as equal political societies, from an equal vote in both branches; the others would risk every consequence rather than part with so dear a right." Bedford said: "The large States dare not dissolve the Confederation. If they do, the small ones will find some foreign ally of more honor and good faith to take them by the hand." Patterson: "New Jersey would never confederate upon the plan before the committee; she would be swallowed up first." Luther Martin: "No modifications will reconcile the smaller States to any diminution of their equal sovereignty." New York was suspected (unjustly, no doubt) of arming in view of possible contingencies. At this junction, Sherman interposed: "We are now at a full stop; nobody, I suppose, means that we shall break up, without doing something; a committee is likely to hit upon some expedient." As the Convention, without dissent, agreed with Gorham, "that the States, as now confederated, have, no doubt, a right to refuse to be consolidated, or to be formed into any new system," a committee was appointed. It reported, July 5th, a compromise, "That in the second branch each State shall have an equal vote." On the 16th that part of the report was carried by the vote of five States to four. Massachusetts, being divided, did not count; New York, not present, was sure to be added to the majority; and New Hampshire, not yet represented, was equally to be relied on. The next day, Gouverneur Morris moved a reconsideration, which was not seconded, and the nice question of an equitable division of political power among the States, which had so long hampered the Convention, was at rest. The wisdom of the decision became every day more apparent, until the equal vote of the States in the Senate was spontaneously excepted from the power of amendment. Wilson and Madison were not only disappointed, but bitterly dissatisfied, and did not attempt to conceal their feelings. Wilson urged the injustice of a minority of men ruling a majority; and did not yield to the distinction between a majority not ruling and being ruled, the distinction between a limited and an unlimited democracy, to which Ellsworth drew his attention. Earlier in the debate he had been equally inattentive to distinctions, until Johnson was forced to point out to him that "controversy must be endless while gentlemen differ in their grounds of argument, those on one side considering the States as districts of people composing one political society; those on the other considering them as so many political societies. The fact is, that the States do exist as political societies." Johnson's claim of "the fact" was not disputed; there were men in the Convention, as out of it, who thought that one political society only would have been better adopted originally, but none dared to affirm that it had been adopted.

Wilson, the earliest of those who have contended that United States does not mean States united, and that Union does mean nation, was a man of great capacity. He had a fixed idea, proof against facts, and even his own inconsistency. During the belief in witchcraft, "possessed" was the word used to express a demon influence beyond escape when once accepted. He was "possessed" by the idea that the States were or should be considered politically as imaginary beings, numbers, *jure divino* rulers, the realities. He never attempted proof, nor disputed disproof of his theory, but could never long escape its mastery of his mind. In the later days of the Convention, he seemed, judging from his language, to be fully conscious of the fact that States were striving to agree upon the conditions precedent to a new Union. He had heard knotty questions referred to committees that bargains *eo nomine* might be made, he could not fail to have heard the universal admission that only through the consent of States was a Union attainable, and he had not heard a claim that any State owed to another State, or to all the other States, any duty not arising from compact, and not owed by one and all to it; yet in the Convention of Pennsylvania (the first to meet) he could say: "I know no bargains made in the Federal Convention. The proposed government does not rest on contract; the idea of a government founded on contract destroys the means of improvement." As he was the only member in the Convention of his State who had sat in the Convention of the States, and as the debates and action in that body were still a secret, his assertion could not be challenged.*

If any suppose that a sense of a right to unity existed at that time, the record will undeceive them. Nothing in the debates arrests attention more than the absence of that which is now strong, the sentiment of a Union. Gorham said that "the Eastern States had no motive for union but a commercial one. They were able to protect themselves, were not afraid of external danger, and did not need the aid of the Southern States." Butler: "The interests of the Eastern and Southern States were as different as those of Russia and Turkey." Gouverneur Morris: "Such distinction is fictitious or real; if fictitious, let us dismiss it, and proceed with due confidence; if it be real, instead of attempting to blend incompatible things, let us at once take a friendly leave of each other." Ellsworth:

* Wilson may not have been conscious of falsehood; a mind to which a Commonwealth of Massachusetts and a Commonwealth of Pennsylvania could at any time have appeared properly held fictions of the imagination as a mermaid, or a centaur, may have held all that passed in the Federal Convention equally properly an illusion of the senses. Or, he may have believed that "people have a right to private truth from their neighbors, and to economic truth from their families, so as not to be abused by their wives, children, and servants, but have no right to political truth; that the people may as well all pretend to be lords of manors, or possessed of great estates, as to have the truth told them in matters of government." In either or any view, his ought now, of all names, to be the most revered, for Story, Webster, Lincoln, and the lesser lights, have done no more than reiterate his assertions, accept his premises, and repeat his language.

"Under a national government he should participate in the national security, but that was all. He turned his eyes, therefore, for the preservation of his rights, to the State governments." Wilson: "If the Confederacy should be dissolved, he hoped a majority, nay, a minority of States, would unite for safety. He was anxious for uniting the States under one government. He knew that there were respectable men who preferred three confederacies, united by offensive and defensive alliances. Many things may be plausibly said, some things may be justly said, in favor of such a project. He could not concur in it, but nothing could be so pernicious as bad first principles."

The delegates always spoke as business men, occupied upon a business matter, conscious that in this world nothing is given, and that everything, in some way or other, must be paid for. They knew that a partnership of the States for external defense, the protection of person and property from internal aggressions, and the care and conduct of interests which they had in common, was as desirable as it would be beneficial. To equalize the contribution of each State to a common fund was a subject upon which they differed widely, compromised, agreed, and wrote their agreement in (as they supposed) plain English. From the opening of the session to the close, no State made a claim of right to have, or to be, in a Union. Such a claim would have been preposterous in the face of the fact that the Convention was arranging to cut loose from the Articles of Confederation; because under those articles, Rhode Island, which had refused to join the Convention, as well as every other State, had the power to defeat any amendment. Nor does it appear from any utterance that the purpose of the Convention was considered revolutionary. The right of each State to alter a form of government, or make a new one, was held settled international law between the States. The foundation of the new system laid—and to lay it had occupied nearly one third of the time the Convention sat—the superstructure was erected more rapidly, perhaps too rapidly; a little of the antecedent tenacity of Madison would have been fortunate. With the political knowledge then diffused, a government was certain to be composed, as it was, of a Legislature, a judiciary, and an Executive, the system of each State.

The character of an Executive gave the Convention much trouble, and exhausted much time. Upon its nature, its functions, its power, the manner and the agency of election, opinions were widely divergent. As no advantage to any State was involved in any of the several modes suggested, received, reconsidered, rejected, restored, or modified, there was no heat in the discussion, and that plan which was finally adopted was only claimed to be less open to objections than any other. The manner of election has been modified by amendment, and the agency apparently, but not fundamentally, superseded in practice. Although, now, the elector only registers the decision of a party convention, his office may, in contingencies not difficult to imagine, become of vital importance. Foreign influence upon the Executive and the Legislature was an object of dread at that period. With our experience, it now seems to have been an apprehension almost silly. That foreign influence has affected the United States disastrously is true, but its action has not been upon officials, but upon masses. An English habit of political thought has permeated many of the States, eating out, as a corrosive, American ideas; and the habit of thought which may be excellent for England, is, or perhaps more properly was, unsuited to the United States, because the basis of government in the two differs.*

---

* The punishment for stealing the labor of British writers. That part of the population of the Union which reads most, thinks least as Americans.

"From causes which might be traced in the history and development of English society and government, the general habit and practice of the English mind is compromise. No idea is carried out to more than a small part of its legitimate consequences. Neither in the generality of our speculative thinkers, nor in the practice of the nation, are the principles which are professed ever thoroughly acted upon.

"Something always stops the application half-way. This national habit has consequences of very various character, of which the following is one: It is natural to minds governed by habit (which is the character of the English more than any other civilized people) that their tastes and inclinations become accommodated to their habitual practice; and as in England no principle is ever fully carried out, discordance between principle and practice has come to be regarded not only as the natural but as the desirable state. This is not an epigram or a paradox, but a sober description of the tone of sentiment commonly found in Englishmen. They never feel themselves safe unless they are living under the shadow of some conventional thing—some agreement to say one thing and mean another. The English are fond of boasting that they do not regard the theory but only the practice of institutions; but their boast stops short of the truth. They actually prefer that their theory should be at variance with their practice. If any one proposed to them to convert their practice into a theory, he would be scouted. It appears to them to be unnatural and unsafe to do the thing they profess or profess the thing they do. A theory which purports to be the very thing intended to be acted on fills them with alarm. It seems to carry with it a boundless extent of unforeseen consequences."—*J. S. Mill.*

The English are a great people—great because, no matter into how many sects and classes, or by what opinions divided, all worship courage, and "are jealous of any attempt to exercise power over them not sanctioned by long usage and their own opinion of right, and fond of resisting authority when it steps over prescribed limits." This characteristic of Englishmen was the characteristic of the colonists. Their quarrel with Great Britain was upon rights, and rights depended upon words. A claim to extend or vary in the slightest degree the originally received meaning of words is a claim to sport with rights. The first-named characteristic of Englishmen has made gradual but steady growth among the descendants of the colonists, and must soon predominate in all, for if one player may be allowed to slip a card with praise and profit, all must, in self-defense, learn to be sharpers. The names now most revered are those of men who have sought and found escape from the ideas of 1776, and from the intention of the ideas of 1787, and from the literal meaning of the words in which those ideas were conveyed; while the names of those who held that they were "the very things to be acted on" are passing into oblivion, if not into obloquy.

The next question of some difficulty was the ratio of representation in the first branch. Population had been settled as the basis of it, but what constituted population? Two of the Southern States insisted that their slaves were population. Some of the other States contended that they were merely property. Mason, though Virginia would gain by treating them as population, held that it would be unfair to rate them as equal to white men. Gorham settled the contention. The Congress had rated them for the purposes of taxation as three for five, and that seemed to him an equally fair proportion for the purpose of representation. When Massachusetts threw her weight into one of balanced scales, the result was not doubtful, and the compromise she advocated was adopted.

The next sharp discussion was upon the taxation of exports, which was claimed and opposed with equal pertinacity, and was finally excluded by a bargain between some of the Eastern and some of the Southern States, which embraced the importation of slaves, on the one hand, and advantages to the interests connected with navigation, on the other. Virginia, Maryland, and Pennsylvania were eager to have the importation of slaves immediately prohibited, through the power of the Federal Government to regulate commerce. Agreeable as that might be to such States as had a surplus of slaves, of whom the price would be enhanced, South Carolina and Georgia insisted upon an exception to the general power.

The bargain as consummated provided that slaves might be imported until 1808, that a duty might be imposed on the importation, that exports should not be taxed, and that navigation acts might be passed by a majority. Upon the importation of slaves, Virginia and Pennsylvania waxed warm, not merely discussing the point in issue, but the moral and economical effects of slavery. South Carolina and Georgia were firm, and not irritable. They saw, or thought they saw, that their interest required such a supply of labor, and with the practice of the world, up to that period, favoring their views, would not accept the judgment of some other States as superior to their own. They offered, however, to absolve the other States from any obligation to suppress insurrections, if scruple might thereby be appeased.

Connecticut settled the dispute. Ellsworth said: "Let the States import what they please. The morality and wisdom of slavery are considerations for the States themselves. The old Confederation had not meddled with this point, and I can not see any greater necessity for bringing it within the policy of the new one." Sherman reminded the Convention that "the States were now in the possession of that right, and, as the public good does not require it to be taken from them, it is best to leave the matter as we find it." The next question, How many States must ratify before the proposed system could become a government? was settled without much discussion. Seven, eight, nine, ten, and thirteen were suggested; nine found favor, none claiming that any State owed to the others ratification as a matter of comity even, much less of right. Wilson would have been satisfied with the assent of seven;

and King, to prevent the possibility of misinterpretation, moved, and the motion was carried by nine States to one, that the words, "between the said States," be added, after "the ratificatious of nine States shall be sufficient for the organizing this Constitution," so as to confine the operation of the Government to the States ratifying it. Such was the bargain which the people of each State—the then recognized source of power—was invited to accept. Under it, besides the common profit of a more efficient General Government, Massachusetts, Pennsylvania, and Virginia would gain power; New Hampshire, New York, Maryland, and Delaware would lose power; Connecticut, New Jersey, and North Carolina would lose power, and gain commercially; Rhode Island, South Carolina, and Georgia would lose a little more than any of the others.

Hamilton and Madison have been termed the architects of the Constitution. Upon that point Hamilton shall speak for himself: "He had been restrained from entering into the discussions by his dislike of the scheme of government in general, but he meant to support the plan to be recommended, as better than nothing." Madison had been overruled upon the principal points he favored. To those two, however, the Convention is due; and, in addition, the very able advocacy of a compact which disappointed them, and the ratification of it by their respective States, absolutely, through their personal exertions. Though all the States aided in building, Connecticut was the architect. Her delegates were pre-eminently reasoners and debaters. They kept the Convention to the basis of facts, to its purpose, trade, to the certainty that no State would take glass beads for money, and that all must give to get.

The Convention would seem to have made a mistake in not providing for the erection of tribunals *pro re nata* to pass upon any issue of good faith between States—good faith having always been understood to be essential to the peace, if not to the continued existence, of any Federal system. In the plan of Confederation prepared by Drayton, in 1778, the necessity was appreciated, and a method exhibited. The omission appears more remarkable, as the two latest, and comparatively recent, civil convulsions in England had turned on that very point of good faith, and had demonstrated the necessity of an arbitrator between the States upon such a subject. Ship-money was an undoubted prerogative of the crown, but for a special purpose; the use of it for general taxation was one of the offenses of Charles I. The dispensing power was an undoubted prerogative of the king; the use of it to circumvent law was the offense of James II. The use of power allowed for certain purposes by a Constitution, for purposes not allowed by that Constitution, is a similar offense of a State against a State; for the right of any control at all, being authorized upon certain subjects only, the desire of control upon other subjects, is latent hostility, and the attempt to exercise control upon them through the Federal organism, avowed hostility. It is a claim to have all the rights peace has given, with all the rights war can give.

Had the Convention been asked why it had not added such tribunals to those provided, it would have answered: For all questions arising under the written paper, tribunals exist; for questions arising outside the written paper, like that between Great Britain and the colonies, the States have announced a rule of decision which this body has no jurisdiction to revise. As men thought at the time, the answer would have been held conclusive; but were it permitted to men to be as wise for the future as for the present, the Convention would have considered that fifty years later the belief of their day might be the heresy of posterity, and have supplied an umpire for that contingency. The Convention was made up of men—Hamilton, Wilson, Morris, Reed, and some others not so outspoken—who thought a government "an impossible government" unless unlimited power was placed by any system in the central organism; of Patterson, Bedford, Luther Martin, Lansing, and some others, who believed a government an impossible government unless unlimited negative power was in any system left in a State; and of men outnumbering both, who believed a system practical and excellent which limited the General Government, the State governments, and the source of all power, the population of a State, and they succeeded in persuading the others to allow the experiment to be tried. Their reasoning, as it may be perceived in the debates, was this: In projecting a system of government, especially one in which liberty is an object of desire by the governed, the point of departure from which the calculation of probabilities starts, is the fact of human nature, that "every human being is born with a Pope in the belly,"* and will not deny himself the luxury of self-will, unless reason points out danger, or some power threatens with punishment. In a monarchy, or in an aristocracy, those who exercise power may feel a sense of and a fear of personal responsibility, they may suffer mediately or directly. In a democracy a voter exercises power, and, as he has no accountability for its use, is freed from fear; while if evil results from his action, and that of those who thought as he thought, and did as he did, his agency is so infinitesimal that he can not have a sense of responsibility. Therefore, in a democracy only such subjects ought to be submitted to suffrage in which all, so far as the condition of humanity permits, have a common interest. If this were true of a single democracy, *a fortiori*, it must be true of conjoined democracies; for if there be association restraints upon a man in his own democracy, they are not operative upon him for another democracy.

---

* The phrase dates from the controversy between Charles I and Parliament.—*Harleian Miscellanies.*

So reasoning, the Convention did what it intended to do, supposed it had done, and said that it had done, in its report to Congress—"fully and effectually vested in the General Government of the Union the power of making war, peace, and treaties; levying money, regulating commerce, and the corresponding executive legislative and judicial functions." Had it imagined that in the future politics in the Union could turn upon amending or not amending the Constitution by majorities, or even by pluralities—for such has been the claim and effect of construction—some method of arbitrating that claim would have been inserted,* or, more probably, the States would have retained the veto power of the Articles of Confederation; for amendment is very strictly guarded. It is all that the mutual jealousy and fear of the small and of the large States would allow: these would not consent that amendments should be proposed by fewer than two thirds of both Houses, practically two thirds of the population of the Union; nor those, that they should be accepted by fewer than three fourths of the States. If every other clause of the Constitution failed to show that a Rhinocracy was not intended, the amendment clause would suffice. At that period it was hoped by many, if not believed by all, that the United States had solved the problem of ages; that they had in their system distinguished so broadly between a right of management and a right of rule, and had marked so clearly the duty of a citizen of one State to the citizens of other States, that the average intelligence and honesty of men could not err therein. But a system, the exponent of the political education of those who make it, can not retain its character-

* The value of arbitration in such cases is not so much that any opinion shall prevail, as that the point of honor shall be saved. The most dangerous disputes are on the point of honor, for then compromise is inapplicable. The Electoral Commission saved the point of honor between two political parties, and was only meant for that purpose.

istics, if the political education of those who subsequently administer it is dissimilar. Then the execution will be at variance with the design. In many of the States of the Union the political education of the masses has for two generations been carefully confined to one line in the Declaration of Independence, and one line in the preamble of the Constitution, both misrepresented by the leaders, and misunderstood by their followers. The result is, that within less than a century the Constitution has become exactly what they who framed it, and they who accepted it, neither understood it to be, nor meant it to be—a Government of numbers, by numbers, for numbers, instead of a Government of States, by States, for States. In politics, mankind seems destined to tread in a circle, from absolutism to limitation, from limitation to absolutism.

THE CONVENTION OF MASSACHUSETTS.

SIXTY-FIVE delegates had been appointed to the Federal Convention, of whom ten had not appeared, having declined the duty, or resigned the office. Thirty-nine attested that the Constitution had been adopted by the unanimous vote of the States present. Had Yates and Lansing been at their posts, the unanimous consent would not have heralded its consideration; sixteen declined to give even such a limited sanction. Their motives were various. Some held that the Convention had exceeded its powers, and that they had no right to assent to more than their delegation of power warranted; others, that there were defects in the plan, and that acceptance or rejection, in the least degree, belonged exclusively to their constituents; others, that signing would bind them, in honor, to an advocacy which duty forbade. The form of attestation had been devised by Gouverneur Morris, to disarm the scruples known to exist, and Dr. Franklin was selected to move its adoption; which he did, in some happy phrases, marked by that sense of the relation of values which had distinguished his life, public and private:

"There are some parts of the Constitution which I do not, at present, approve, but I am not sure that I shall never approve them. The older I grow, the more apt I am to doubt my own judgment and to respect the judgment of others. I sign this Constitution with all its faults, if there are such, because I think a general government necessary for us, and because there is no form of government but what may be a blessing to the people, if well administered. I believe further, that this government is likely to be well administered for a course of years, and can only end in despotism, as other forms have done before it, when the people shall become so corrupted as to need despotic government, being incapable of any other. I doubt if any other convention may be able to make a better Constitution; for when you assemble a number of men to have the advantage of their joint wisdom, you inevitably assemble with those men, all their prejudices, their passions, their errors of opinion, their local interests, and their selfish views. It therefore astonishes me to find this system approaching so near perfection as it does; and I think it will astonish our enemies, who are waiting to hear that our councils are confounded, and that our States are on the point of separation, only to meet hereafter for the purpose of cutting one another's throats. I consent to this Constitution, because I expect no better, and because I am not sure that it is not the best. The opinion I have of its errors I sacrifice to the public good. I have never whispered a syllable of them abroad. Within these walls they were born, here they shall die. If every one of us, in returning to his constituents, were to report the objections he has to it, and endeavor to gain partisans in support of them, we might prevent its being generally received, and thereby lose all the salutary effects and great advantages resulting naturally in our favor among foreign nations, as well as among ourselves, from a real or apparent unanimity. Much of the strength and efficiency of any government depends on opinion; on the general opinion of the goodness of the government, as well as of the wisdom and integrity of the governors."

If the Constitution was to take effect upon its adoption

by the Convention, the reasoning of Franklin would have been incontrovertible, and a sense of any defect would have been properly confined to subsequent efforts for amendments in the mode it permitted; but if it was to be judged by others, whether they were not entitled to all the information they could get, was a very different question, and a very nice and difficult question of political ethics. If a man commissions another to buy him a horse, the balancing in the mind of the agent of the merits and demerits of the animal need not be communicated; but if he asks that the purchase be recommended, he expects that defects will be disclosed, as well as qualities extolled. But is the rule which would govern, in such a case of private trust, applicable in its full extent to a public trust? Is there not an element in one which can not exist in the other—the *salus populi* of the considering State? Upon this point of political morality a long and acrimonious debate occurred in the Convention of New York between Hamilton and Lansing. Unfortunately, it is not reported, for any conclusions of a mind so fertile as that of Hamilton would be of inestimable value. The charge of Lansing was: "You think this Constitution very defective; so do I. I state my objections; you conceal yours, and only utter praise. You are insincere to those who favor, and unjust to those who oppose this instrument." The answer of Hamilton probably embraced the entire range of political duty and morality, and, if so, left certainly no point untouched. He must have discriminated with the nicest skill, between differing duties under differing circumstances, and asserted the right of judgment upon probabilities. If, from what he could gather, he had become satisfied that nine States would ratify, that conviction would dictate one course; if he had not, another line of action might be proper, and the geographical position and relative importance of probable ratifying and non-ratifying

States must be an element of consideration and judgment; or, if the choice lay, not between what he thought good, but what he thought possible, the possible should be commended exclusively; finally, if there was only an option between bad and worse, good sense would forbid him to inveigh against the bad. Whatever his reasoning, it convinced the body he addressed. A similar attack was made in the Virginia Convention upon Randolph, who, refusing to sign, urged and voted for ratification. His answer was frank and full: "I refused to sign, because I saw grave defects in the Constitution. I felt that it was my duty then; I still think it was. My opinion as to the existence of those defects has not changed. But eight States have ratified. A Union must be formed. It is better for Virginia to be in that Union, in spite of defects in the Constitution, than to be out of it in consequence of them. For every other act of my life I appeal to the mercy of God; for this, I am content to rely on his justice." Debates in the conventions of five States are reported, how fully or fairly it is impossible now to say. If Johnson, reporting Parliament, took care "that the Whig dogs should not have the best of it," lesser men, if they had prejudices (and who is without them?), can not be hoped to have been perfectly impartial. In his notes of the debates in the Federal Convention, in spite of his claim to complete accuracy, it is certain that the hearing of Madison was more acute for what he wished said, than for what he wished unsaid, and, if contemporaneous documents may be trusted, he did not quite hear all that was said. Enough (perhaps all that is necessary) is preserved, to display the general sense of men upon some points, and their differences upon others, and to testify to the intelligence of the delegates to those conventions, and of the constituencies which appointed them. Nothing can convey a better idea of the political interest and activity, than a remark of a delegate in the Convention of

Massachusetts. That body was very large, there being on the average a representative for each thousand souls: "When this Constitution was published, my town met to examine it; we studied it for seven hours; then we all agreed that it would not do." Massachusetts was the pivotal State. If she had not ratified, it is certain that Virginia and New York would have followed her example; New Hampshire most probably would not have ratified; North Carolina did not, and Rhode Island could not be counted on. Either a second Convention must have met, perhaps, under less happy auspices, or the States might have separated, some gravitating to Massachusetts, some to Virginia, and some to Pennsylvania. Therefore the debate in her Convention is of primary importance. It is marked by moderation in tone, calmness even in pertinacity, and respect for opposition. The first question mooted was the biennial representation to the House. Habit has great power. The delegates to the Congress of the Confederation were elected for one year, were subject to recall, and compelled to rotation. A change in that respect not unnaturally excited suspicion, and demanded justification. Fisher Ames sought to disarm the one, and supply the other: "I consider frequent elections one of the first securities of popular liberty, in which its essence may be supposed to reside. How shall we make the best use of this instrument? A delegation of power for a single day would defeat the design of representation; an election for a term of years would be repugnant to it. The period must be so long that the representative may understand the interest of the people, yet so limited that his fidelity may be secured by a dependence on their approbation. Because annual elections are safe, it does not follow that biennial are dangerous. Both may be good. Besides, the term, being fixed by the Constitution, is not subject to repeal. We are sure it is the worst of the case.

Upon its own merits, however, it meets my entire approbation. First, from the extent of territory to be governed, as large as that of Rome in the zenith of its power; next, from the objects of legislation, if few, national; two years will be necessary to enable a man to judge of the trade and interest of the State he never saw; lastly, for the more perfect security of our liberty, for faction and enthusiasm are the instruments by which popular governments have been destroyed. The people always mean right, and, if time is allowed for reflection and information, always do right. Biennial elections are a security for the sober, second thought. A member chosen for two years may feel some independence. The factions of the day will expire before his term." The astuteness of the "plain men," who questioned the propriety of the change, is not less noticeable than that of the more educated class. If the territory is so extensive, and the interests so complicated, a member can only be competent from thorough previous study. We shall elect men who know, not men who have to learn. If the objects of legislation are few, little time will be necessary; if they are national, a common feeling will make them easy. As for faction, that is as probable of a second as of a first year. The arguments of Ames and others prevailed, and experience has justified their conclusions, but not for the reasons they gave. A member who has served one term, is worth, as a public man, twice as much as a successor of equal ability. By that time, he has begun to know the House, and the House to know him. The clause which gives to the Congress the power to regulate the time, place, and manner of elections was vigorously attacked and not very vigorously defended. The defense was twofold: That a State might neglect or refuse to make the necessary regulations, and thus, no representatives being elected, the General Government would be dissolved; that it would operate as a check upon the Federal Senate, and its constituents, the State Legislatures, and in case of the invasion of a State, act, when its Legislature might be powerless. Secondly, the improbability that the power would be abused. To the former, the rejoinder was, why not add, "if a State shall neglect or refuse"? that will prevent prevarication. To the latter, which had been warmly urged by a clergyman, you preach human depravity in the pulpit, and human infallibility on this floor. The clause had passed in the Federal Convention with little discussion and no dissent, but in the State Conventions was viewed by many as a source of probable injustice, and possible collision. An exclusive Federal regulation would have been consistent with the scope of a scheme, which aimed to separate as distinctly as possible the functions of the general and State governments. Against that, no argument could be urged, which could not be urged against any other delegation of power, but, if it was desirable that a State originally should exercise it, a subsequent intervention would necessarily be partisan. There may be good reasons for the clause, but the fanciful ones asserted in the Convention, and the equally fanciful idea of Madison, that there would be a continuous inherent hostility between the Federal and the State Legislatures, have little weight in themselves and have found no warrant in experience. In all constitutional governments, and pre-eminently in a federal republic, discretion as to rights ought to be excluded to the very limits of possibility, for liberty consists less in what a man has, than in what none can take from him. To the objection that slaves were made an element of representation, King answered: "The principle of this Constitution is that taxation and representation go hand in hand. The apportionment was the language of all America." He, with others, contended that, in the bargain, the advantage in that respect was with the Northern States. Upon slavery itself, the opposition insisted that the Constitution pledged them to it, and to the slave-trade besides; for under the Confederation, as all admitted, the connection was between States, not between the people of the States; whereas, under the plan submitted, there would be not only a constitutional government, but a constitutional people, and if the people of Massachusetts became a part of that people, they would be as fully guarantors of property in slaves as of any other species of property. General Heath answered: "I apprehend it is not in our power to do anything for or against those who are in slavery in the Southern States. I detest the idea of slavery. It is generally detested by the people of this Commonwealth, and I ardently hope that the time will soon come when our Southern brethren will view it as we do, and put a stop to it, but we have no right to compel them. Two questions naturally arise, if we ratify the Constitution. Shall we do anything by our acts to hold the blacks in slavery? Shall we be partakers in other men's sins? Surely not, for in nothing do we voluntarily encourage the slavery of our fellow-men." Others dilated upon the fact that a power over the slave-trade, not before possessed, was acquired. It is impossible to suppose that the Convention did not know of the bargain by which the carrying States, without giving up anything they had, got a great deal they had not, a limitable slave-trade being one of its conditions. The next ground of attack was the tenure of the Senate, which Ames thus vindicated: "It is necessary to premise that no argument against the new plan has made a deeper impression than that it will produce a consolidation of the States. This is an effect all good men will deprecate. The State governments are essential parts of this system, and the defense of this article is drawn from its tendency to their preservation. The senators represent the sovereignty of the States; in the other House individuals are represented. The Senate may not originate bills. It need not be said that they are principally to direct the affairs of war and treaties. They are in the quality of embassadors of the States, and it will not be denied that some permanency in office is necessary to the discharge of their duties. If they were chosen yearly, how could they perform their trust? If they were brought by that means more immediately under the influence of the people, they will represent the State Legislature less, and become the representatives of the people. The absurdity of this, and its repugnancy to the federal principle of the Constitution, will appear more fully, by supposing that senators are to be chosen by the people at large, which, if there is any force in the objection to this article, would be proper. But whom in that case would they represent? Not the Legislatures of the States, but the people. This would totally obliterate the federal feature of the Constitution. What would become of the State governments, and on whom would devolve the duty of defending them from the encroachments of the Federal Government? A consolidation of the States would ensue, which, it is conceded, would subvert the new Constitution, and against which this article, so much condemned, is our best security. Too much provision can not be made against a consolidation. The State governments represent the wishes, the feelings, and local interests of the people. They are the safeguards and ornament of the Constitution, they will protract the period of our liberties, they will afford a shelter against the abuse of power, and will be the natural avengers of our violated rights. This article secures the excellence of the Constitution, and affords just ground to believe that it will be in practice, what it is in theory, a federal republic." The argument of Ames must have compelled general conviction, for that objection was never again seriously pressed. So far, the opposing forces had skirmished; battle was joined upon the taxation and judiciary clauses. The former, it was objected, is "a very good and valid conveyance of all the property in the United States, to certain uses indeed, but those capable of any construction the trustees may think proper to make, and they are not amenable to any tribunal." The general answer was: Government must have all necessary power, the quantum can not be fixed, it must depend upon the exigency which calls for its exercise. It may be abused, that possibility is inseparable from all governments. Somebody must be trusted. Parsons added that there was a perfect remedy against misgovernment within the Constitution. "The people have it in their power effectually to resist usurpation without being driven to an appeal to arms. An act of usurpation is not obligatory, it is not law, and any man may be justified in his resistance. Let him be considered a criminal by the General Government, yet only his fellow-citizens can convict him; they are his jury, and if they pronounce him innocent, not all the power of Congress can hurt him, and innocent they certainly will pronounce him, if the supposed law he resisted was an act of usurpation." It is curious to see the claim of Calhoun forty years later, anticipated by one of the greatest judicial minds Massachusetts ever produced. The rejoinders were: "Faction is the vehicle of all transactions in public life. This truth all know, and also that the prevalent faction is the body. Is it contended that the prevalent body must always be right, and that the true patriots will always outnumber the base and the selfish? Then it must follow that no public measure ever was wrong, for it must have been passed by a majority, and no power therefore ever was or ever can be abused. But if we know that power can be and has been abused, why should we expect more from Congress than from the myriads of public bodies which have preceded it and have abused power? A sovereign power within a sovereign power is not conceivable by the mind. Congress ought to have supreme power over all matters within its jurisdiction, but that jurisdiction ought to be so distinctly bounded that every one may know the utmost limits of it. Where is the Bill of Rights which shall say toCongress, 'Thus far shalt thou go and no farther'?" * The objections to the judiciary may properly be omitted, as amendments justified and obviated them.

The contest nearing a close, Ames called on those who stood forth in 1775, to stand forth now, to throw aside all interested, and party views, and have one purse, one heart for the whole, and to consider that as it was necessary then, so it is necessary now, to unite—or die we must. The appeal brought to the floor one "who would not have troubled the Convention, if they who were on the stage in 1775 had not been called on. I was one of them, a member of the court all the time; if any body had proposed such a Constitution as this, it would have been thrown away; it would not have been looked at. We did not contend with Great Britain for a threepenny duty on tea, but upon a right to tax us, and bind us in all cases whatsoever. Does not this Constitution do the same?"

Debate exhausted, and a decisive vote imminent, it was apparent that the Constitution would be rejected.† But there had been a great deal of neighborly outside discussion among the delegates, and they were possessed of each other's reasonings and feelings as we could not be, if the report was as full, as it is meager. Both sides earnestly desired a Union. One side was so eager for it, as not to stickle at any price; the other side would only pay

* A Bill of Rights can not exclude the success of aggression, but it does exclude the consecration of its success. Posterity will reverse the judgment of former generations.

† King wrote to Madison that in the face of a majority supposed of from eight to twelve, a division upon any point had not been ventured. Another correspondent informed him that, through the proposal of amendments (to be recommended only) a majority of from fifteen to twenty could be secured for ratification.

so much. Those who favored ratification could not lose by paying less for what they wanted, and, if they pledged themselves to amendments embodying the views and obviating the objections of the others, must not all be satisfied? Hancock was selected to offer the compromise, which he did with equal skill and courtesy: "My situation has not permitted me to enter into the debates of the Convention. It appears to me, from what has been advanced in them, that it is necessary to adopt the form of government proposed, but observing a diversity of sentiment among the gentlemen of the Convention, I have frequently conversed with them on the subject, and from those conversations I am induced to inquire whether the introduction of some amendments would not be attended with the happiest consequences. I am unable, if my abilities would permit, to go more largely into the subject, and I rely on the candor of the Convention to bear me witness that my wishes for a good Constitution are sincere. I submit a proposition to your consideration, with the desire and hope that it may tend to promote a spirit of union." The proposed amendments read, Samuel Adams moved that they be taken into consideration: "I have had my doubts of this Constitution. I could not digest every part of it as easily as some gentlemen. This is my misfortune, not my fault; other gentlemen have had their doubts. I have observed the sentiments of men as far as Virginia, and from newspapers, and in the conventions, I find the same doubts, but in my opinion the proposition submitted will have a tendency to remove such doubts and to conciliate the minds of the Convention, and of the people out-of-doors." Bowdoin, one of the strongest advocates of ratification, expressed his "hearty approbation of the propositions of his Excellency, as they would have a tendency to relieve the fears and quiet the apprehensions of some very worthy and respectable people." A motion for a committee of two from each county, to consider the amendments proposed, and any others that might be suggested, and report thereon, was carried unanimously. The amendments reported met universal favor. Adams admitted that the first article was "a summary of a Bill of Rights, and consonant with the second of the Articles of Confederation." Dr. Jarvis, a zealous and most powerful supporter of ratification, termed it a "positive security of what is not expressly delegated, leaving nothing to the uncertainty of conjecture, or the refinements of implication, an express reservation of what is nearest and most agreeable to the people." The end, however, was not yet reached. Upon the point whether ratification should be conditional upon the acceptance of the amendments, or absolute with a recommendation of them, the unanimity was dissolved, the contest was renewed, and the issue was again doubtful. The opposition claimed that the power of the Convention only extended to ratification or rejection, Conditional ratification was legitimate, but the mere proposal of amendments was not contemplated in their appointment, nor embraced in their duties. Dr. Jarvis answered: "Under what authority are we acting, from Congress, from the Federal Convention, from the State Legislature? From neither, from the people of Massachusetts as their immediate representatives to execute the most important trust it is possible to receive. Are not the people of Massachusetts, assembled by their delegates, at liberty to resolve in what form that trust shall be executed? To what tribunal are we amenable? Only to God and our own consciences. It appears to me that a conditional ratification is equivalent to a total rejection. As so many other States have received the Constitution as it is, how can it be made to appear that they will not adhere to their resolution, and should they be as warmly and pertinaciously attached to their opinions, as we might be to ours, a long and painful interval might elapse before we should have the benefit of a Federal Constitution. Will the States which have recently adopted, consent to call a new convention at the request of this State? If nine should ratify, are we going to expose this Commonwealth to the disagreeable alternative of being forced into compliance, or of remaining in opposition? Why these amendments should not be adopted I can not conceive. They are general, not local, not calculated for the particular interest of this State, but with indiscriminate justice, comprehend the circumstances of the man on the banks of the Savannah and on the margin of the Kennebec. The remaining seven States will have our example before them. There is a high probability that they, at least some of them, will take our conduct as a precedent, perhaps they will assume the same mode of procedure." Ames summed up with his usual ability: "Almost every one who has appeared against the Constitution, has declared that he approves it with the amendments. One distinguished for his zealous opposition would hold up both hands for it, if they could be adopted. I admire this candid way of discussing the subject, and shall endeavor to treat it with equal care and fairness. The nature of the debate is totally shifted. The inquiry now is, as to the degree of probability, that the amendments will be incorporated in the Constitution. What, in any future thing, do we devise more than the probable? What more is another Constitution? All agree that we must have one. If we ratify, and a union is formed, nine States only have to agree; if we do not, and a union is not formed, thirteen States have to be satisfied. Either in a union the amendments will be accepted, or they will not. If we believe that they will, we ought to be unanimous for ratification; if we believe that they will not command the assent of enough States, this State ought to submit, for one eighth or one tenth of the people ought not to dictate to the whole." The mass of opponents were not convinced, and were angry. They felt that a little of the *pia fraus* had been used, that the offer of amendments, not of the possibility, or probability of amendments, averted a vote of rejection. Their mood is discernible in the report, though discreetly veiled, but their bitterness at those who, over the narrow bridge of probability, were about to pass from one camp to another, is less dimly seen. When all who wished to be heard, had been gratified, Hancock rose to put the question. He prefaced it with a short address, of which the close is perfect in temper and pertinency: "Let the question be decided as it may, there can be no cause for triumph on one side, or chagrin on the other. Should there be a great division, every good man, every man who loves his country, so far from exhibiting extraordinary marks of joy, will sincerely lament the want of unanimity, and strenuously endeavor to cultivate a spirit of conciliation both in the Convention and at home. The people of this Commonwealth are a people of great intelligence in public business. They know that we have none of us an interest separate from theirs, that it must be our happiness to conduce to theirs, and that we must all rise or fall together. They will, therefore, never forsake the first principle of society, that of being governed by the voice of the majority. Should the proposed form of government be rejected, they will zealously attempt another. Should it, by the vote now to be taken, be ratified, they will quietly acquiesce, and, where they see want of perfection in it, endeavor in a constitutional way to have it amended." The report upon which the vote was to be taken can not be omitted:

"Commonwealth of Massachusetts in convention of the delegates of the people of the Commonwealth of Massachusetts, 1788.

"The Convention having impartially discussed, and fully considered, the Constitution for the United States of America, reported to Congress by the convention of delegates from the United States of America, and submitted to us by a resolution of the General Court of the said Commonwealth, passed the twenty-fifth day of October last past, and acknowledging with grateful hearts the goodness of the Supreme Ruler of the Universe in affording the people of the United States an opportunity deliberately and peacefully, without fraud or surprise, of entering into an explicit and solemn compact with each other, by assenting to and ratifying a new Constitution, in order to form a more perfect union, establish justice, insure domestic tranquillity, provide for the common defense, promote the general welfare, and secure the blessings of liberty to themselves and their posterity, do, in the name and behalf of the people of the Commonwealth of Massachusetts, assent to and ratify the said Constitution for the United States. And, as it is the opinion of this Convention that certain amendments and alterations in the said Constitution would remove the fears and quiet the apprehensions of many of the good people of the Commonwealth, and more effectually guard against an undue administration of the Federal Government, the Convention do recommend that the following alterations and provisions be introduced into the said Constitution:

"1. That it be explicitly declared that all powers not expressly delegated by the aforesaid Constitution are reserved to the several States to be by them exercised.

"2. That there shall be one representative to every thirty thousand, according to the census mentioned in the Constitution, until the whole number of representatives amounts to two hundred.

"3. That Congress do not exercise the powers vested in them by the fourth section of the first article, but in cases where a State shall neglect or refuse to make the regulations therein mentioned, or shall make regulations subversive of the rights of the people to a free and equal representation in Congress agreeably to the Constitution.

"4. That Congress do not lay direct taxes, but when the moneys arising from the impost and excise are insufficient for the public exigencies, nor then, until Congress shall have first made a requisition upon the States to assess, levy, and pay their respective proportions of such requisitions agreeably to the census fixed by the Constitution, in such way and manner as the Legislatures of the States may think best; and in such case, if any State shall neglect or refuse to pay its proportion pursuant to such requisition, then Congress may assess and levy such State's proportion, together with interest thereon, at the rate of six per cent per annum, from the time of payment prescribed in such requisitions.

"5. That Congress create no company with exclusive advantages of commerce.

"6. That no person shall be tried for any crime by which he may incur an infamous punishment or loss of life, until he be first indicted by a grand jury, except in such cases as may arise in the government, and the regulation of the land and naval forces.

"7. The Supreme Judicial Federal Court shall have no jurisdiction of causes between the citizens of different States, unless the matter in dispute, whether it concern the realty or the personalty, be of the value of three thousand dollars at the least; nor shall the Federal judicial powers extend to any action between citizens of different States, when the matter in dispute, whether it concern the realty or the personalty, is not of the value of fifteen hundred dollars at the least.

"8. In civil actions between citizens of different States, every issue of fact arising in actions at common law shall be tried by a jury if the parties or either of them request it.

"9. Congress shall at no time consent that any person holding an office of trust or profit under the United States shall accept of a title of nobility or any other title and office from any king, prince, or foreign state.

"And the Convention do in the name and in the behalf of the people of this Commonwealth enjoin it upon their representatives in Congress, at all times, until the alterations and provisions aforesaid have been considered agreeably to the fifth article of the said Constitution, to exert all their influence and use all reasonable and legal methods to obtain, a ratification of the said alterations and provisions in such manner as is provided in this said article."

The pledges of the Convention were not kept. When the amendments were submitted to the States, the vote of Massachusetts was not given for them. They became part of the charter of government by the vote of States which had accepted the ideas of Massachusetts, and followed her example. The piety of the Commonwealth must have obtained, for its respectability, a divine dispensation from good faith.

The count showed 187 yeas, 168 nays. The shifting of ten votes had been sufficient. The statistics of the votes are curious, interesting, and perhaps instructive. The delegates from some counties voted almost unanimously yea; from others, with the same degree of unanimity, nay. The officers of the late war, by about three to two, voted nay; the clergy, by about five to one, voted yea. The bench, the bar, and the trading and commercial classes, almost to a man, voted yea. The yeomanry as a class voted nay. Why the yeomanry were so determined in opposition is a question easily answered. They had suffered and fought for seven years to establish a fact, and a political principle. The fact, that Massachusetts was a community, and, as such, entitled to say what were her rights and maintain them; the principle, that the obligation of governor and governed is reciprocal and the right of judgment equal—those things they had looked for in the Constitution, and had not found them, or, if there, not so distinctly stated as to defy denial. The first amendment they thought supplied the deficiency, but they would not trust amendment to any contingency. The reiterated assurances of a set of checks and balances, within the system did not impose upon them for a moment. They knew that the electors, not the elected (whether State Legislature, Congress, or a President), were the real depositories of power. That power was what they wanted defined and bounded. They knew that unless there was a check upon that, "constitutional government is but solemn trifling, all trusts in a Constitution being grounded on the assurance not that the depositories of power will not, but that they can not, misemploy their power." They understood liberty to be, as Fisher Ames defined it, "due restraint upon the liberties of others." Such due restraint they knew was necessary to keep them from injustice to others, and others from injustice to them. They did not propose to change masters, and to give to a Union the right they had denied to Great Britain. In every other convention men of trained abilities were pitted against each other. In that of Massachusetts all her disciplined intellect, familiarity with debate, wealth, and high social position were on one side; on the other, the laborers in peace, and the rank and file in war. Whoever appreciates political insight, must see, from the scanty record, that her yeomanry were indeed "a people of great light."

THE CONVENTION OF VIRGINIA, 1788.

The report of debate in the Convention of Virginia, which exceeds six hundred pages, discloses three great currents of opinion: One, that the Constitution was acceptable upon its merits; one, that it was not, but indispensable; and one, that it would be, if amended, though not until amended. The former was in a minority; even with the addition of the second a majority was doubtful, and, if tradition may be trusted, only in the closing days of the Convention were the few votes necessary to ratification secured; and then only by an abandonment of the pretensions which at the outset had characterized its advocates. The amenity so conspicuous in the Convention of Massachusetts is less apparent in the Convention of Virginia; but the circumstances were not the same. Massachusetts had a question almost abstract to resolve; if she rejected, a preponderance of strength and wealth would have responded to her decision. If Virginia rejected, the only ally to be counted on was North Carolina. The issue, therefore, was no longer simple; the dangers of disunion, as well as the merits of an instrument, had to be weighed, and the friends of adoption, standing on vantage-ground, were little disposed to conciliation. The question forces itself upon the mind, why men almost universally satisfied with the structure of the proposed government, content with the apportionment of influence among the States, craving a Union, and possessing the same objects of political desire, divided into parties, almost hostile. The discord can not be accounted for merely as a recurrence of the historical fact that in religion and in politics men who agree upon ninety-nine out of one hundred points, are sometimes dogmatical, indeed fanatical, upon the single point, and, paradoxical as it sounds, are the farther apart the nearer they are together, because, the less that is to be yielded, the more each thinks that the other ought to give way. There were two causes, one of which lies on the surface, and one which will appear in this debate. Unfortunately, the Federalists, early, as can be seen in the letters of the very moderate Madison, arrogated to themselves a monopoly of Unionism and patriotism; and if they did not distinctly designate themselves, as Cicero did his party, the Good, came dangerously near the thought, and its expression. As human nature is constituted, they could scarcely do otherwise, under their intense conviction that then was the golden moment, that the opportunity lost could never be regained, that the rejection of the Constitution must be followed by anarchy, and anarchy by inter-state wars, to a common destruction. The anti-Federalists, principally consisting of the less timid classes in each State, held such fears to be preposterous. They knew that there was then a Union, and they believed that it would continue to exist, that it must exist, because its advantages were palpable to every man and every State. They did not believe that it could depend upon any one special set of words, but upon a sense of its benefit, or, if it could, that the Constitution was that special set of words, and they felt that the assumption of a lack of patriotism, or Unionism, in an opposition to any proposed Constitution, was an affront; that the reason Mason gave in the Federal Convention for refusing his signature—"I will not say take this, or nothing"—was their reason, and while they were satisfied to vest in a Federal Government every power necessary to a Union, they were determined to have nothing but a Union, and resolved that every expression in the Constitution should be so precise and clear, that a possibility of doubt, or pretext for quarrel, should be excluded. When Mr. Lincoln said that "the human mind can not reach to the audacity of denying any right plainly written in the Constitution," he spoke the praise, although the epitaph, of the policy which sought to have every right and power plainly written.* Possibly it is a matter of regret that the criticism of the anti-Federalists had not been more minute and searching, and their emendation more thorough. War, and the change of the principle of government from consent to force, might have been averted. With such parties existing, the debate in the Virginia Convention opened. Among the debaters were men whose names are inseparable from the history of the United States—Madison, Henry, Marshall, Monroe. With these were associated others, perhaps not inferior in mental power, if less fortunate in opportunities for displaying it. The preamble and first article having been read in the Committee on the Whole, Nicholas rose to commend it. He reviewed the plan of representation in its different characteristics; the qualification of electors, of those they might elect, the number, tenure of office, and powers of the latter; and, lastly, the security of the people. The qualification of electors for the general and State Legislatures was the same; a reasonable provision, as the qualifications of electors varied in the States. The qualifications of the elected were age and residence; one, requisite for maturity of judgment, the other for an identity of interest with a State. The term of office, neither too long nor too short, conciliated duty to the Union, with responsibilty to constituents for intelligent and faithful service. The number had to be fixed arbitrarily at first, but

* The right not only plainly written in, but the Constitution itself is, freedom from control the rule, control the exception, the characteristic of governments based on consent: in those not so based, control is the rule, freedom from control the exception.

upon the disclosures of a census would be altered to exactness. So far as the security of the people might be involved, the House had a greater weight in the system than the Commons in that of England. The Commons had overmatched greater powers than the House would have to encounter, and their responsibility to constituents was less. This power so vested can not be abused, for experience has proved that men can trust those whose rights are identical with their own. Still more, the people being possessed of the supreme power, can change the Government when they please. The power to regulate the time, manner, and place of elections for Federal officers in the House, he deemed to be indispensable; without it there could be no security for the General Government against the hostility of State Legislatures. If a State Legislature, by accident or design, failed to regulate, the inaction would eventually put an end to the Union. Again, there might otherwise be as many different periods of election as States; therefore, without a power in the Federal Government to prescribe uniformity, a full House might be unattainable. Henry inquired of the delegates to the late Federal Convention what was the purpose of that body; what did it mean by "We the people" instead of "We, the States?" Did it design a great consolidated government? Randolph seized the opportunity to deny vacillation. He had refused to sign because he thought amendments necessary. Had this Convention met at an earlier date, he should have thought them a condition of acceptance. Now it was too late; the hope of subsequent amendments was all that was left to him. The objection to "We, the people," was the least and most trivial of all possible objections; it carried its answer with it. Should not the people be consulted upon the construction of a government by which they were to be bound?

Mason claimed that direct taxation, before requisition

made and refused, in which case it would be proper, subverted every principle hitherto maintained, and would make the system a consolidated Government. The plan he had hoped for, was one which would draw a line between the General Government and the State governments so distinct as to prevent that clashing of interests and powers, which must otherwise end in the destruction of one or the other.

Pendleton admitted that a consolidated government—"one with sole, exclusive, and unlimited power, executive, legislative, and judicial—would be inadmissible; but the Constitution was neither such, nor could by any possibility be made such. It only extended to the general purposes of a Union, and did not intermeddle with the local particular affairs of the States. The Federal Government depends upon the existence of the State governments; without those, to continue the existence of Congress, and preserve order and peace within their boundaries, it must be destroyed. Fault has been found with the expression, 'We, the people.' If the objection means that a union ought not to be of the people, but of the governments of the States, the choice of words is very happy. What have the State governments to do with the Constitution? If they were to determine upon acceptance, the people would not be the judges of the terms on which it was adopted. Direct taxation encounters objection. A government must be supported; for support it must have its own revenue. If it had to depend upon requisitions, precious time might be lost between its necessities, and possibilities of supply through the action of the State governments. Requisitions might be neglected, even refused; collision might ensue, and the Union be dissolved."

Henry rejoined: "The fate of America is involved in my question. Whether this plan is a confederation of States, or a consolidation of States, turns upon that little 'We, the people.' The inquiry is not how trade may be increased, or a great and powerful people may be formed, but how liberty—which ought to be the direct end of government—may be secured. Unfortunately, nothing will preserve it but force. To give up the means to preserve it will be ruin. My great objection to this government is, that it does not leave us the means of defending our rights. It is said that it is not safe to reject it. Why not? It is said that there is a plain way of getting amendments. Am I mad, or are my countrymen mad? Six tenths of the people of four States, not one twentieth of the American people, can deny the most necessary alteration. The gentleman who presides (Pendleton) tells us that to prevent abuses in our governments we will assemble in convention, recall our delegated powers, and punish our servants for abusing their trust. There would be fine times if, to punish tyrants, it were sufficient to assemble the people! The arms will be gone, and neither an aristocratic nor a democratic spirit be left. In what nation was a revolution ever heard of, compassed by those without any power at all against those with power? There will be a standing army. How can that be punished? Will your mace-bearer be a match for a disciplined regiment? What will be the situation? Power of direct taxation unbounded and unlimited, power of exclusive legislation over ten miles square, and over all places purchased for the erection of forts, magazines, arsenals, and dock-yards is conceded. What resistance could be made? The attempt would be madness; the country would be in the hands of enemies, their garrisons in its strongholds. Even the discipline of the militia is to be alienated. Will the oppressor let go the oppressed? Was there ever such an instance? Can the annals of mankind exhibit one single example when rulers, overcharged with power, let the oppressed go upon their most urgent entreaty? Sometimes the oppressed have got loose by one of those bloody struggles which desolate a country; but a willing relinquishment of power is one of those things of which human nature never was, nor ever will be, capable. The first consideration should be liberty; the second, union. Are not the means confounded with the end in this government? There is no responsibility, no punishment for the grossest maladministration, for the most outrageous violation of immunities. By what law can aggressions be punished? None is visible. The preservation of liberty depends upon the chance of men being virtuous enough to punish themselves."

Randolph pressed the consideration of safety: "Were I convinced that our accession was not necessary to preserve this Union, I would not accede without previous amendments, but I am satisfied that it will be lost if we reject. The Union is necessary to the safety of Virginia, and indispensable to her happiness. I confess that it is imprudent for one nation to form an alliance with another whose situation and construction of government are dissimilar; but can Virginia exist without the Union? She can not, as I will prove." He detailed the reasons for his belief that she would not be capable of defense against the bordering States, if they should be hostile, and that they would be hostile, he justly inferred from human nature.

Madison was "pained to hear continual distortion of the natural construction of language. It was enough for any human production to bear a fair discussion. If powers be necessary, apparent danger is not a sufficient reason against conceding them. Since the general civilization of mankind there had been more instances of the abridgment of the freedom of the people by the gradual and silent encroachments of those in power than by violent and sudden usurpation. The history of ancient and modern republics showed their destruction to have resulted from turbulence, violence, and the trampling of the rights of a minority by a majority. On consideration of the peculiar situation of the United States, and the causes of the diversity of sentiment which pervaded their inhabitants, there is great danger that the same causes may terminate in the same fatal effects they had produced in other republics. That danger ought to be wisely guarded against, and perhaps in the progress of this discussion it might appear that the only possible remedy for those evils, and the means of protecting and preserving the principles of republicanism, would be found in that system which is declaimed against as the parent of despotism. The principal question is, whether the proposed government be federal or consolidated. It is of a mixed nature, in a manner unprecedented. There is not an express example in the experience of the world. It stands by itself. In some respects it is of a federal nature, in others of a consolidated nature. In the manner in which the Constitution is investigated, ratified, and made the act of the people of America, it is not completely consolidated nor entirely federal. Who are the parties to it? The people, but not the people as composing one great body, but the people as composing thirteen sovereignties. No State is bound by it without its own consent. Should all the States adopt it, it will be a government established by the thirteen States of America, not through the intervention of Legislatures, but by the people at large. In this respect, the distinction between the existing and proposed system is very material; that was created by the dependent, derivative power of the Legislatures of the States, this will be by the superior power of the people. This same idea is in some degree attended to in the provision for alterations. A majority of the States can not introduce amendments, nor are all required for that purpose. Three fourths must concur. In this there is a departure from the federal idea. The members of the House of Representatives are to be chosen by the people at large, in proportion to the numbers in the respective districts. The Senate is elected by the

States in their equal and political capacity. Had the government been completely consolidated, the Senate would have been elected by the people in their individual capacity. Thus it is of a complicated nature, and the complication may be hoped to exclude the evils of an absolute consolidated government, as well as those of a mere confederacy. If Virginia were separated, her power and authority would extend to all cases; if all powers were vested in the General Government, it would be a consolidated government; but the powers of the General Government are enumerated. It has legislative powers on defined and limited objects, beyond which it can not extend its jurisdiction. If any of those powers be necessary, inconvenient though they be, Virginia must submit to receive them, or to lose the Union. Direct taxation will probably be unnecessary for the general purposes of government, but in case of war every resource must be at its command."

Corbin considered Madison's definition of the proposed government exact, and its appropriate designation, "a representative federal republic, as contradistinguished from a confederacy. It placed the remedy for disorder in the hands that felt it, not as the other, in the hands that caused it. The evils justly complained of in popular governments —faction, dissension, and the consequent subjection of the minority to the caprice and arbitrary decision of the majority—will be excluded by the Constitution, for faction must be less when the interest of a nation is entirely concentrated, than when it is entirely diversified. This government, which will make us one people, which will have a tendency to assimilate our situations, and which is so admirably calculated to produce harmony and unanimity, can not possibly admit of an oppressive combination by one part of the Union against the other. Therefore, what end will be answered by an attempt to obtain previous amendments? Will the States that have adopted rescind their resolutions? Had we adopted, would we recede to please the caprice of another State? Must there not be another Federal Convention? Must there not be another convention in every State? If our conditions are rejected, we must be excluded from the Union, or other conventions must be called, eternally revolving and devising expedients without coming to a final decision. Let us go hand in hand with Massachusetts, adopt and propose amendments." Henry resumed: "We are told that this government, taken collectively, is without example; that it is national in this part, federal in that; in the brain it is national, in the stamina federal; some limbs are federal, some national; it is federal in conferring powers, it is national in retaining them; it is not to be supported by the States, the pockets of individuals are to be searched for its maintenance. What signifies the most curious anatomical description of it in its creation? To all the common purposes of legislation it is a great consolidation of government, but, when it works sorely on our necks, we may have the consolation of knowing that it is a mixed government, and of saying that it was federal in its origin. Is it not absurd to adopt this system, and to rely upon its being afterward amended? Is the rage for novelty so great, that you are first to sign and seal, and then retract? You are to bind yourself hand and foot, for what? To be unbound. You are to go into a dungeon, for what? To come out. Is there no danger, when you go in, that the bolt of federal authority will shut you in?" Lee answered: "This new system shows, in stronger terms than words could declare, that the liberties of the people are secured. Its principle is, that all powers are in the people, and that rulers have no powers but what are enumerated in that paper. When a question arises with respect to the legality of any power assumed or exercised by the Congress, it is plainly on the side of the governed. Is it enumerated in the Constitution?

If it be, it is legal and just; if otherwise, arbitrary and unconstitutional." Monroe stated distinctly the ground upon which many who recognized the superiority of the Constitution in most respects to the confederation, and were desirous to adopt it, felt compelled to insist upon a previous amendment: "Power is divided between the State and Federal Governments. It is distributed in the Federal Government, for better administration, between three branches; there is little danger of either being subverted by the others, but, if the Federal Government and a State differ as to the boundaries of power, there is very great danger that their coalition, for they will naturally coalesce, may subvert the rights of the people. Where is the security for rights? where is a check within the system? I can not see any. There ought to be a third distinct branch, to maintain an equilibrium." Though no immediate answers were made to Monroe, two were incidentally attempted in the course of debate. Madison found a solution of the difficulty in the virtue of the people: "If they were not virtuous enough, and intelligent enough, to elect men of virtue and intelligence, no theoretic checks or forms of government could insure." The experience of the world is directly opposite. The nature of a government may make bad men better, or good men less good. If the application be narrowed to republican governments, or, still more, restricted to the United States, the statement is just as untenable. If a theory of government is, that rights and duties are reciprocal and coextensive, the character of men will be higher than if it fails in that respect. If the theory of a government admits of a penalty for disregard of duty, each succeeding generation will become more and more self-controlled. If there be no penalty, each succeeding generation will become less and less self-restrained. Marshall supposed the solution to be found in the independence of the judges. But he, like Madison, evaded the question. Independence is not impartiality. The appointing power necessarily has a bias, it selects for a judge a man known to have the same bias. It can not be otherwise, whenever the construction of a constitution is the basis of parties. A Protestant would not be willing to submit the points on which he differs from the Church of Rome to the decision of the College of Cardinals, eminent as that body may be; nor would a Roman Catholic, to the Bench of Bishops in England, or to a synod of Presbyterian divines, strong as might be the intellect, pure the nature, and just the intention of the bishops and divines. What makes the impossibility of freedom from bias in a Federal judiciary more striking is, that nominally Federal officials are the parties appointing, but the real party is the political will of some of the States. The question of Monroe—"What prevents a coalition, and with a coalition, what becomes of rights?"—remains unanswered.

Marshall followed: "The supporters of the Constitution idolize democracy. They admire the system, because they think it establishes a well-regulated democracy. What are the favorite maxims of a democracy? Strict observance of justice and public faith, from which no mischief or misfortune ought to deter, and a steady adherence to virtue. The friends of the Constitution are as tenacious of liberty as its enemies. They desire no power in the Government to endanger it, only such as will protect and preserve it. What are the objects of the national Government? To protect the United States in war, and to promote the general welfare. It must have powers commensurate with its objects, and the right of direct taxation is so essential, that without it the plan may as well be rejected. It is said that there are no checks; what has become of the American spirit? In that source, upon oppression, will be found the check and control. In this country there is no exclusive personal stock of interest. The interest of the community is blended and inseparably connected with that of the individual. When he promotes his own, he promotes that of the community; when he consults the common good, he consults his own. Such checks abound. Is it an absurdity to adopt before amendment; is the object of adoption, solely amendment; is it not, besides, safety, protection from faction? If, on trying the system, amendment shall be found necessary, what restrains amendment? The Government is not supported by force, it depends on our free-will. When experience shows us any inconvenience, we can correct it; but until we have experience on the subject, amendments, as well as the Constitution, are to try. There is such a diversity in human minds, that it is impossible we should concur in one system until we try it."

In the remarks of Marshall there is a statement which may have been justified by personal knowledge, but of which neither proof nor probability can be found in any recorded utterance. To him, in the Virginia, as to Wilson, in the Federal Convention, peculiar information on the matter seems to have been conveyed: "There are in this State and in every State many who are decided enemies of the Union. Reflect on the probable conduct of such men. What will they do? They will bring in amendments which are local in their nature, which they know will not be accepted. Disunion will be their object. This will be attained by the proposal of unreasonable amendments."

Mason and Henry were strenuous opponents of unconditional ratification; both were among the foremost men of their time, long in public life, and from official positions brought in contact with numbers. Mason's testimony on the point is explicit and full: "Foreigners would suppose, from the declamation about the Union, that there was a great dislike in America to any General Government. I have never in my whole life heard one single man deny the propriety and necessity of a Union. This necessity is deeply impressed upon the American mind. There can be no danger of any object being lost, when the mind of every man in the country is strongly attached to it—to the blessings of a Union, I hope, not merely to the name. They who are loudest in praise of the name, are not more attached to the reality than I. The security of our liberty and happiness is the object we ought to have in view in seeking to establish a Union. If we endanger, instead of securing those, the name of Union is a trivial consolation. We ask such amendments as will point out what powers are reserved to the State government, and clearly discriminate between them, and those given to the General Government, so as to prevent future disputes and the clashing of interests. Grant us amendments to that end, and we will cheerfully with our hands and hearts unite with those who advocate the Constitution, and will do everything we can to support and carry it into execution."

Henry was not less emphatic: "The reality of Union, not the name, is the object which most merits the attention of every friend of his country. The American Union is dear to every man. Every man with three grains of information must think and know that Union is the best of all things. Let it be shown that the rights of the Union are secure, and we consent."

Words may be false, but facts can not mislead. No amendment was ever sought that was not general, and no amendment proposed had any object but peace and liberty.

Grayson held the radical defect of the Constitution to lie in the opposition of its component parts. "There are two opinions in the world upon the construction of governments—one that men can govern themselves, the other that they can not, but must be ruled by some force independent of them. I believe in the possibility and advantage of self-government. If I am right, a system should be purely federal; if I am wrong, a system should be a complete consolidation, in which case the object to be sought was a yoke as light as possible. The proposed plan was too strong for a federal, and too weak for a consolidated government. Republican in form, it was founded on the principles of a monarchy, with the three estates, but without the inherent checks of the British monarchy. Its executive was blended with legislative functions, contrary to the opinion of the best writers, and, fettered in some parts, was as unlimited in others, as a Roman dictator. Its democratic branch was marked with strong features of aristocracy, and its aristocratic branch with the impurities and imperfections arising from inequality of representation and want of responsibility. The Constitution did not remove the fatal inconvenience of clashing State interests. The members of Congress from Virginia would be actuated by the interests of the State; so would those from every other State. I hope my fears may be groundless, but I believe, as I do my creed, that the operation of the system will be a faction of seven States to oppress the rest of the Union. It may be said that we are represented. Will that lessen our misfortunes? A small representation gives a pretense to injure and destroy. The British would have been glad to take us into the Union, like Scotland, giving a small representation. The Federal Convention, called to remedy the defects of the Confederation, was asked for bread, and has given a stone. What was the defect of the Confederation? No means of a revenue. Supply that defect by giving it the control of commerce, and as other defects become apparent apply, by a mode of amendment, the remedy. Apportion the public debts so as to throw the unpopular ones on the back lands, call only for requisitions for the interest on the foreign debt, and aid them by loans. Keep on so, till the American character is marked with some certain features; we are too young to know what we are fit for. The continual migration of people from Europe, and the settlement of new countries on our Western frontier, are strong arguments against making new experiments in government now. In framing a government, the genius and disposition of a people, and a variety of other circumstances, ought to be considered.

But we are told that unless we adopt this Constitution we shall be disunited and ruined forever, that we shall have wars and rumors of wars, and that every calamity shall attend us. Pennsylvania and Maryland are to fall on us from the North, like the Goths and Vandals of old; the Algerines, whose flat-sided vessels never come farther than Madeira, are to fill the Chesapeake with mighty fleets to attack us on the front; on the rear the Indians are to invade us with numerous armies, to turn our cleared lands into hunting-grounds; and the Carolinians from the South, mounted on alligators, I presume, are to come and destroy our corn-fields and eat up our little children. These dangers are merely imaginary, and ludicrous in the extreme. Are we to be destroyed by Maryland and Pennsylvania? For what will democratic States make war? How long since have they imbibed a hostile spirit? But the generality is to attack us. Will they attack us after violating their faith in the first Union? Will they not violate their faith if they do not take us into their confederacy? Have they not agreed by the old Confederation that the Union shall be perpetual, and that no alteration shall take place without the consent of Congress, and the confirmation by the Legislatures of every State? I can not think there is such depravity in mankind as that, after violating public faith so flagrantly, they should also make war on us for not following their example. We are told that we ought to take measures, which otherwise we should not, for fear of disunion. Disunion is impossible. The Eastern States hold the fisheries, which are their corn-fields, by a hair.

They have a dispute with the British Government about their limits at this moment. Is not a general and strong government necessary to their interests? If ever nations had inducements to peace, the Eastern States now have. New York and Pennsylvania anxiously look forward to the fur-trade. How can they obtain it but by union? Can the Western posts be got or retained without union? How are the little States inclined? They are not likely to disunite. Their weakness will prevent them from quarreling. Are not the inducements to union strong, with the British on one side and the Spaniards on the other? Thank Heaven, we have a Carthage of our own!"

Grayson protested against direct taxation. His mind could not conceive of two powers equally supreme over one object. Madison observed "that requisitions were not only an awkward and roundabout way to attain a desired result, but were more calculated to insure inequality and dissatisfaction than direct taxation. Men will pay less grudgingly if certain that every one must pay, but with the possibility that some may escape payment, all must be reluctant. The experience of the Confederation was conclusive against them. Besides, in case of war, some States would be more exposed to its evils than others; imports would be less productive and expenses increased, and the more secure any State was, the less it would feel the exigency which compelled requisitions. There was another consideration which might be operative in the future. As manufactures increased, the revenue from imports would diminish, and the vacuum must be filled by direct taxation. So far as a cession of power was involved, there was no augmentation, simply a change necessary to the efficacy of a power already vested in the Confederation. The difference was not in a theory of government, but in the practice of government. Taxation to the same extent, and for the same purposes, was authorized by both systems, but one made a State the tax-payer, the other individuals. The first had proved ineffectual, the latter would be adequate."

Pendleton had "studied the Constitution; not, however, hoping to find a scheme free from the possibility of objections. That could not be expected of a human effort. He did see the seeds of disunion in it, though in the future, not the immediate operation of the Government, but he trusted to the power of amendment to extrude those agencies. He could not see any difficulty in the duality of governments, their spheres of action being totally different, one embracing interests common to all the States, the other interests peculiar to each State. They ran on parallel lines; if each kept to its own sphere, they could not conflict. Direct taxation might never be necessary, but it might become indispensable to the safety of the Union, and therefore the power of direct taxation ought to be possessed by the General Government. He desired amendments as earnestly as others, but Virginia had no right to ask the adopting States to accept conditions; she should put herself in the same position as those States; then her attitude would be conciliatory, and the amendments she craved would be unmistakably in the interest of all."

Grayson having remarked that manufactures were the resource of a redundant population, crowded into a limited space; that the extent and fertility of the territory would for many years attract labor almost exclusively to agriculture; that therefore imports must be more productive, and consequently that direct taxation could not be necessary, and its exercise might become a source of friction; Madison admitted that "imports would increase until population became so great as to compel a recurrence to manufactures, but the unsettled parts of America would be inhabited at no distant period. In twenty-five years the population in every part of the United States would be as great as it then was in the settled parts; already, wherever there was a medium, manufactories were beginning to be established. In preparing a government for futurity it should be founded on principles of permanency, not on conditions of a temporary nature. Direct taxation could not be a cause of friction. When the authority of the General Government was exclusive, no question could arise; when it was concurrent, future legislation must regulate action. It was necessary, however. Men have to pay for the advantages of government, and it obviously could make no difference to them whether they pay to the Federal Government directly, or through the conduit of a State; but, to the public credit of the Union, the difference was very great whether its debts were to be paid from its own resources, or whether payment depended upon the compliance of thirteen bodies. No one would lend it a shilling on that contingency."

Henry rejoined: "We are told that all powers not given, are retained. Advert to the history of England. Its people lived without a declaration of rights till the war in the time of Charles I. Power and privilege then depended upon implication and logical discussion. Upon the expulsion of the Stuarts, a Bill of Rights prescribed to William of Orange on what terms he should reign, and the end of construction and implication was the end of revolutions. Did Scotland enter into a union with England and trust to subsequent amendments? No; all the terms of the bargain were settled beforehand. We are told that our safety is secured by representation. Is Virginia represented? Rhode Island and Delaware together, infinitely inferior in extent and population, have double her weight, and can counteract her influence. Representation, therefore, is not the vital principle of this Government." He inquired why the States were not to pay their own agents, why the salaries were not fixed, and why members of Congress should be permitted to abandon an office to which they had been elected by their constituents, for one to which they had not been designated. "If incitement to office was desirable, the provision was proper; if not, it should be corrected by an amendment."

Madison developed the reasoning of the Federal Convention: "If compensation had been appointed by the State governments, the Government of the Union would not have been safe; at least its existence must have been precarious, with members of the Congress dependent upon salaries from other public bodies competent to withhold them. The salaries had not been fixed, because the purchasing power of money varies; and if they had become inadequate, the door would have been open to evils from inadequacy, which reflection must suggest as probable. This was the most delicate point in the organization of a republican government, the most difficult to establish on unexceptionable grounds. It appeared to him that the Convention had fixed on the most eligible; the Constitution takes the medium between two extremes, and perhaps with respect to the eligibility of representatives to office, with more wisdom than either the British or the State governments. They can fill no new offices created by themselves, nor old ones of which they have increased the salary. If they were excluded altogether, it is possible that disadvantages might accrue from the exclusion, not to mention the impolicy and injustice of denying them a common privilege. They will not relinquish their legislative, to accept other offices. They will more probably confer them on friends or connections. If this be an inconvenience, it is incident to all governments."

Grayson objected to the right of the Senate to propose or concur in amendments to money bills. "Practically it was equivalent to originating them."

Madison answered that, in his view, a right of the Senate to originate money bills was unimportant, and, if it had been given, would not have been objectionable. Its power of amendment was commendable. Without that, the slighest exceptionable feature might cause the rejection of a bill, and all the time spent and labor bestowed would be wasted. As an alteration can not conclude the House, no harm was possible, many advantages might be gained, and the rights and interests of the States be better guarded.

Mason stated an amendment which ought to be made in that clause of the Constitution which confers the power to arm and discipline the militia: "I wish an express declaration that in case the General Government shall neglect to arm and discipline the militia, the State governments may. With this single exception I would agree to this part." Madison "could not conceive that, by giving that power to the General Government, the Constitution had taken it from the State governments. The power is concurrent, not exclusive. Does the organization of the government warrant a belief that the power will be abused? Can that be supposed of a government of a federal nature, consisting of many coequal sovereignties, particularly as it has one branch chosen from the people?"

Henry observed: "If you give too little power to-day, you may give more to-morrow; but if you give too much power to-day, you can not retake it to-morrow; for that purpose to-morrow will never come. If you have the fate of other nations, you will never see it. It is assumed that American rulers will not depart from their duty. It is a universal principle, in all ages and all nations, that rulers have been actuated by private interest; equally so will they be in America. In a sense of duty you will not find a check. If the power of arming and discipline is concurrent, the power of naming officers must be concurrent. To admit this mutual concurrence will carry you into endless absurdity, the Congress with nothing exclusive on one hand, nor the States on the other."

Nicholas confuted the argument: "The power of arming and disciplining is already vested in the State governments, and, though given to the General Government, is not given exclusively, because in every instance where the Constitution intends that the General Government shall exercise any power exclusively, words of exclusion are particularly inserted. Consequently, in every case where such words of exclusion are not inserted, power is concurrent, unless it is impossible that the power should be exercised by both the General Government and the State governments. It is not absurd to say that Virginia may arm the militia if Congress neglects to arm them, but it would be absurd to say that Virginia should arm them after Congress had done so, or to say that Congress should appoint the officers and train the militia when it is expressly excepted from their powers."

Marshall closed: "Each government derives its powers from the people; each is to act according to the powers given it. The State governments do not derive powers from the General Government; then, must not every power be retained which is not parted with? If a power, before in the State Legislatures, is given to the general Legislature, both shall exercise it, unless there be an incompatibility or negative words precluding the State governments. All the powers which the States possessed, antecedent to the adoption of the Constitution, of which they are not divested by any grant of, or by any restriction from, in the Constitution, they must necessarily be as fully possessed of as ever they had been."

Henry was not yet satisfied. "The nations which had retained their liberty were comparatively few. America would add to the number of the oppressed, if she depended on constructive rights and argumentative implication. If rights not given were retained, why were there negative clauses upon some of the powers of Congress? Concurrent power is not reducible to practice. If there was an insurrection in Virginia against the State, and an insurrection in another State against the General Government, the call of one or the other must be obeyed. Of which?" Madison replied: "The power must be vested in Congress, or in the State governments, or there must be a division, or there must be a concurrence. If in the State governments, where is a provision for the general defense? If it must be divided, let a better method be shown. When the militia are in the service of the United States, the United States govern them. What can be more positive than that the States govern them when not? A State is not barred from calling forth its militia to suppress insurrections and domestic violence; and, in its right to call for Federal aid, it has a supplementary security."

What is the intent, it was asked, of the power to call forth the militia to execute the laws of the United States? Is a military government aimed at? The answer was, the meaning is plain—if the civil power be insufficient. Why not say so? was the rejoinder; we are all agreed upon that point, and, when the expression of a purpose is so easy, why leave a loop-hole for construction? On the face of the instrument there is nothing to exclude the danger of a future claim that the words mean exactly what they say, and no more. Madison answered by recalling "a remark which had fallen from a gentleman on the same side as himself, and which deserved to be attended to. If we be dissatisfied with this national Government, and choose to renounce it, this is an additional safeguard to our defense."

Great objection was made to the exclusive jurisdiction over the ten miles square. Madison thought he had obviated it, by the suggestion that the Federal Government could not otherwise be guarded from the undue influence of some State, or be safe in its deliberations, and secure from insult. He pointed out that there must be a cession of the land by a State or States, which could settle the terms of cession, and make such stipulations as they pleased.

Grayson said: "There are no objections to giving all necessary powers, but there are objections to giving any unnecessary powers. Exclusive jurisdiction might be held to nullify, within that district, provisions of the Constitution which had been considered sagacious. Governmental and police powers would answer all the ends proposed to be attained. No check could be found in terms of cession or stipulations, for the ten miles square might be located in a Territory."

"That objection fails," answered Nicholas, "for the power of Congress over the Territory is limited to making rules and regulations for its disposal; the grant of it was for the benefit of all the States, it can not be perverted to the prejudice of any." Pendleton argued that "the clause did not by any fair construction give Congress any power to impede the operation of any part of the Constitution, or to affect the rights of the citizens of the Union. The jurisdiction is not opposed to the general powers of the Federal Legislature, or to those of the State Legislatures. It is opposed to the legislative power of the State within which the ten miles square are situated. It does not go one step beyond the delegated powers."

Upon almost every clause of the Constitution, as it was read, one point was raised, or one question reiterated. Where is the distinct acknowledgment that all power not conceded is retained? Where is there a word to foreclose the assertion that it is not? At this time you believe and say, with perfect sincerity, not only that it is, but that the mind can not conceive that it is not, but can you answer for the future? In every other system, government has every power not expressly excluded. If, hereafter, men shall contend that this system is to be gauged by the rules applicable to other systems, what, so far as reasoning goes, is to confute them? You construe to-day, why shall not others construe to-morrow? What is to prevent "general welfare" or the "sweeping clause" being held in the future, absolute surrenders of every right, and an investiture of complete sovereignty. There is a clause in the Articles of Confederation reserving to each State every power, jurisdiction, and right not expressly delegated to the United States. That clause met general approval. Why was it not inserted in the Constitution? Would it have consumed too much paper? What was the motive for omitting it, or what could be the objection to adding it?

Mason stated that he was the more pertinacious upon this point, because he had perceived in the Federal Convention the disposition, and, moreover, the intention, on the part of some, to extend power by construction, so that by slow, gradual, incessant encroachments, the Constitution could be made, not what it purported to be, or was then represented to be, but what they thought it should have been.

Madison, unlike some great men of his party, sincere in advocacy and sanguine in hope, demanded an explanation. Mason answered, "The fact is well known that the disposition was not merely prevalent in the Federal Convention, but that it exists in many men in every State of the Union, among whom are men of great abilities and high character. From frequent intercommunication with Madison, he knew that such were not his sentiments, and he believed that they were not entertained by any delegate from Virginia." Madison was satisfied with the disclaimer as to himself, but it does not appear that he denied the accuracy of the statement as to others. From the political action in the earlier years of the republic, the disposition might have been then so inferred; but from this debate we learn that the anti-Federalists were possessed of the views and objects of their opponents. It is now easy to account for the intensely bitter party spirit, and the fierce hatreds and fatal encounters of individuals. Few things irritate men more than the sense of trickery, intended or attempted.

Nicholas reasserted what his side had frequently asserted: "The sweeping clause" has the same effect and no more as if it had followed each delegation of power, and was bounded as a summary of them. The "general welfare" was united to the particular power of levying and collecting taxes, etc., and was not connected with any general power of legislature. The question had been put, why negative words were found in the Constitution? They created exceptions to a general power; for instance, under the power to regulate commerce, the slave-trade might at once have been prohibited, but for the exception. To the question, How is the extent of power to be determined? he answered: "By the same power, which in all well-regulated communities determines the extent of legislative powers. If a Legislature exceeds its powers, the judiciary will declare the excess void, or the people will have the right to declare it void. It is universally agreed that the people have all power; if they part with any, is it necessary to declare that they retain the rest?"

Mason denounced the clause which admitted a slave-trade. He "would have preferred to it a Union excluding the States which exacted it. Slavery was a great misfortune; only one could be greater—manumission." Henry equally deplored slavery, and dreaded manumission. These sentiments appear to be contradictory, but they are not. An abolitionist in a slaveholding community is such from his reason, not his emotions. His aim is to reconcile, not to antagonize, the present and the future with the past. He recognizes his duty to the master as a fellow-citizen, to the slave as a fellow-man. Duty to the master was held to be the higher, as the obligation to him was twofold, whence his consent must be coaxed or bought. Duty to the slave was held to consist not merely in freedom from thrall, but in betterment of existence. Therefore all the early abolitionists, and they were many, considered that abolition and colonization must go hand in hand. They believed that of two free races, inhabiting the same country, intermarriage being repugnant, one must finally be extirpated. They did not believe that intermarriage was among the possibilities of the future, basing their opinion on the example of the colonists, who shunned that relation with the Indians, though then white women were scarce, and red women comely. This generation is either better or wiser, but as the learned, the pious, the liberal Dr. Arnold, not many years since, thought the difficulty insuperable, it may be indulgent to the mistakes of its ancestors.

Madison "would conceive the clause impolitic if it were an evil which could be excluded without encountering greater evils. The Southern States would not have entered into a union without that temporary permission; and if excluded, the consequences might have been dreadful to them and to us. We are not in a worse situation than before. The traffic is prohibited by our laws, and the prohibition may be continued. The Union in general is not worse off, for, in the Confederation, the importation might be continued forever, while now, it may be forbidden after twenty years. Great as the evil is, a dismemberment of the Union would be greater; those States, if disunited, might solicit and receive aid from foreign powers."

Mason claimed "that a separate clause in the Constitution ought to settle distinctly the status of property in slaves. Any species of property exclusively held by some of the States, which the other States neither wanted nor would want, must have a safeguard; for, if it may be assumed that men may be trusted to govern others, when they themselves will suffer from misgovernment, it does not follow that they are capable of just power when others only bear the evils of injustice. Federal taxation might be so used as to destroy the value of slave-property. The right of reclamation of the fugitive slave was of little importance; the meaning was that the fugitive should not be protected." It may be doubted if then there was a man in the United States who conceived that "delivering" was a State duty, much less a Federal duty. The anti-Federalists at least understood the phrase to mean that in every State, process of law for the recovery of property should be as applicable to property in men, as to property in things. When the political idea was dominant that the Federal Government would be the stronger the more it meddled, the fugitive-slave law was passed, and its constitutionality was affirmed judicially, upon that political theory, not upon history or language.

Madison answered that the Southern States most affected were satisfied, and dreaded no danger to their property. The extent to which the General Government could intermeddle with slavery was levying a tax of ten dollars a head upon importations, and prohibiting the slave-trade after a fixed period.

It was suggested that the vice-presidency was a useless office, attended with possible dangers, besides giving some one State a greater representation in the Senate.

Madison disclosed the reasoning of the Federal Convention on the subject. Some officer was necessary to continue the Government in case of an accident to the President; and a casting vote, in case of a tie, was a desirable legislative expedient. He added that, as the Vice-

President would probably be always selected from one of the larger States, the inequality, which was excessively slight, would be least inequitable.

Inquiry made, why in a certain contingency, the President was to be elected in the House, by a vote of States, Madison answered that it was the result of a compromise between the larger and the smaller States.

Pendleton opened the debate upon the judiciary clause. His opinions carried great weight, from his judicial experience. He was satisfied, except with the expression "law and fact," which he admitted to be unfortunate. The authority of Congress over "exceptions and regulations" relieved him, however, from an anxiety he should otherwise feel.

Mason agreed that in cases affecting diplomatic agents, in controversies between States, between citizens of the same State claiming land under grants from different States, and in admiralty and maritime questions exclusive Federal jurisdiction was proper; and equally so, with some restrictions, in controversies to which the United States were parties. In disputes between a State and citizens of another State, a foreign state, its citizens or subjects, Federal jurisdiction was manifestly improper. He objected to the word "arising," as vague, ambiguous, and inconsistent with any conception of limitation. Anything might be said to arise under a constitution.

Henry added: "There never seems to be any difficulty in finding apt words for grants of power, but, for the security of liberty, language is apparently only capable of ambiguity. Are the judiciaries and citizens of all the States so lost to shame as to be incapable of justice? Is an individual to summon a State before a court, especially a foreigner? Was it ever heard of that such a privilege should be given a foreigner? Was war to enforce the judgment of a court? Congress, it is said, may be trusted to make such exceptions and regulations as experience will suggest. It is not the business of representatives, but of conventions, to settle the basis of government. Why can not a State be trusted to do justice between a citizen and an Englishman or Frenchman? The provision is disgraceful; it will degrade the judiciary, and prostrate the Legislature of Virginia."

Madison asked the committee to consider the difficulties in organizing a government for the United States. "They who prepared the paper on the table found difficulties not to be described. Mutual deference and conciliation were absolutely necessary. It was settled, when no party was formed, no particular propositions made, when the minds of men were calm and dispassionate; yet even under such circumstances agreement upon a general system was very hard to be attained. The judiciary clause claimed the indulgence of a fair and liberal interpretation. He would not deny that more accurate attention might place in it terms which would remove some of the objections which had been made; but with a liberal construction there was nothing dangerous nor inadmissible. Surely it was not supposable that an individual could drag a State into court; the only operation of the clause will be, that a State must sue an individual in a Federal court. Perhaps disputes between citizens of different States had better have been left to the courts of the States."

Marshall considered this part of the plan a great improvement on the system about to be abandoned. "There are tribunals for the decision of controversies, before not at all, or improperly provided. The opposition is based upon the idea that the Federal courts will not determine causes with the same fairness and impartiality as other courts. Why not? Why do we trust judges? From their appointment and independence in office. Will not the judges in the Federal courts be chosen with as much wisdom as the judges in the State courts? Will they not be equally, if not more, independent? If there is as much wisdom and knowledge in the United States as in any one State, will not that wisdom and knowledge be exercised in the selection of judges? Why conclude that they will not decide with the same impartiality and candor? It is said that it is disgraceful that the State courts shall not be trusted. Does the Constitution take away their jurisdiction? It is necessary that the Federal courts should have cognizance of cases arising under the Constitution and laws of the United States. What is the service and purpose of a judiciary, but to execute the laws in a peaceable, orderly manner, without a recurrence to force, conflict, and bloodshed. To what quarter can you look for protection from an infringement of the Constitution if power is not given to the judiciary, no other body can afford such protection. It is objected that Federal officials may be secured from merited punishment by Federal courts. What bars the injured from applying for redress to the State courts? It is objected that a State may be called to the bar of a Federal court. The intent is to enable a State to recover claims against individuals residing in other States. It is said that it would be partial to allow a suit by a State, and not against a State. It is necessary, and can not be avoided. There is a difficulty in making a State defendant, which does not prevent its being plaintiff. Objection is made to suits in the Federal courts by the citizens of one State against the citizens of another. Were I to contend that it was necessary in all cases, and that the Government would be defective without it, I should not use my own judgment; but is not the objection carried too far? What can they get more than justice? It has been urged that we ought not to depend upon others to rectify defects which it is our duty to remove. Our duty is to weigh the good and the evil before we decide. If we be convinced that the good greatly preponderates, though there be small defects, shall we give up the good, when we can remove the little mischief?"

Grayson answered: "The excellence of human nature has been invariably urged in all countries when the cession of power was in agitation. It seemed to be the basis of all the arguments on one side. The judiciary clause is so vague and indefinite in expression that human nature can not trace the extent of its jurisdiction, nor ascertain its limitation. Between the Federal and the State courts the line should be so distinctly drawn that interference will be impossible, otherwise there can be no arbiter but the sword. The judiciary itself is upon as corrupt a basis as the act of man can place it. The salaries may be increased. That a State may be sued by or sue a foreign state is a new law of nations. Consent must be had, it is said. The foreign state must consent, the American State must submit. Is it not so written in the Constitution? Congress, we are told, will eliminate defects. If it can not make a law against the Constitution, neither can it make a law to abridge the Constitution, and the judges can neither extend nor abridge it."

Randolph, "though he could not concur with those who thought the judiciary clause so formidable, must admit that the words used to define jurisdiction were ambiguous in some parts, and unnecessarily extensive in others. 'What are cases in law and equity, arising under the Constitution? What do they relate to? The phraseology is very ambiguous, and can carry jurisdiction to an indefinite extent.' He thought that the intent of one clause was, that a State might be sued by an individual, and approved of it; any objection which might be obviated by honesty had with him little weight. If he was asked why, knowing the Constitution to be ambiguous, he would vote for its ratification, he answered, because it contains within itself the means of removing defects, because he believed that any defects would be removed, and because he believed men capable of honesty, even under temptation. If he did believe that all power not expressly retained, was parted with, he would detest the system; therefore he proposed that Virginia should ratify, putting in the form of ratification the words that all authority not given is retained by the people, and may be resumed when perverted to their oppression; and that no right can be canceled, abridged, or restrained by the Congress or any officer of the United States. Those words he supposed would manifest the principles on which Virginia adopted the Constitution, and entitled her to consider the exercise of a power not delegated a violation of it."

Henry replied: "He saw the dangers which may and must arise if the Constitution was accepted. There could be no reliance on it for rights and liberties. There will be an empire of men, not of law. Rights and liberties would depend upon men. Their wisdom and integrity may preserve, their ambitious and designing views may destroy. Already it must be seen that the friends of the Constitution do not agree as to its meaning. A Constitution ought to be so clear as to be comprehended by every man." Wythe admitted the imperfections of the plan and the propriety of amendments, but the excellency of many parts could not be denied by its warmest opponents. Experience, the source of improvement in the science of government, could alone develop consequences. He proposed ratification, and the recommendation of such amendments as were thought necessary. "They certainly must be obtained, as amendments were desired by all the States, and had been proposed by some." Henry urged that the amendment, to the necessity of which every one agreed, "that all power not expressly delegated is reserved," should precede ratification. "To talk of it as a thing subsequent, and not an inalienable right, is to leave it to the casual opinion of the Congress. They will not reason with Virginia about the effect of this Constitution, they will not take the opinion of this Convention as to its operation, they will construe it as they please. Subsequent amendments stand against every idea of fortitude and manliness in a State, or in any one. Evils admitted in order to be removed, and tyranny submitted to, in order to be excluded by subsequent alteration, were things new to him."

Madison claimed great allowance for the plan: "Its friends have never denied that it has defects, but have claimed that the defects were not dangerous. As all are agreed that it has defects, it will be easy to remedy them by the healing power in the instrument itself. Other States have been content to ratify, and rely on the probability of amendments. Why should not Virginia do the same? She has hitherto always spoken with respect to her sister States, and has been listened to with respect. It is neither the language of confidence nor respect to say that she does not believe that amendments for the promotion of the common liberty and general interest of the States will be consented to by them."

Innes took the subtle ground that, "if previous amendments were proposed, the people would not have had an opportunity of expressing their views upon them; whereas, upon subsequent amendments, they would have a facility of examination, and an expression of judgment. He did not apprehend any danger from the dissimilarity of interest, North and South. He could not conceive that with the brotherly affection, reciprocal friendship, and mutual amity, so constantly inculcated, and with the strongest reasons of self-interest besides, the Northern States could be so blind as to alienate the affections of the Southern States, and adopt measures which would produce discontent, and terminate in the dissolution of a Union so necessary to the happiness of all. To suppose that they would act contrary to such principles would be to suppose them not only destitute of honor and of probity, but void of reason; not only bad men, but mad men."

It is apparent that, if the Federalists had profited by the example of Massachusetts, had at once admitted defects, and concurred in amendments, their object would have been gained with little loss of time and great saving of temper. As soon as they yielded what they should have proffered, the Constitution was ratified by 89 yeas to 79 nays. What would have happened, if they had continued obstinate, may be learned by the vote upon a motion to strike out one of the proposed amendments. Although all the great leaders who had championed ratification spoke and voted for the motion, it was defeated by a majority of twenty.

The form of a ratification drawn up by a committee exclusively Federalist—Randolph, Nicholas, Madison, Marshall, and Corbin—contains these words: "The powers granted under the Constitution, being derived from the people of the United States, may be resumed by them, whenever the same shall be perverted to their injury or oppression, and every power not granted thereby remains with them and at their will." As soon as possible after the Constitution became the Government of the United States, the amendments so eagerly desired were imbedded in it. The ninth and tenth meant something to the mind of that generation; to subsequent generations the meaning depended upon degrees of latitude.

THE CONVENTION OF NEW YORK, 1788.

In the Convention of New York, after the preliminaries of order were settled, debate was opened by Livingston (the Chancellor). He directed attention to the fact that throughout the United States one language was spoken, one religion professed, and one political principle recognized—that all power is derived from the people. "It must be of little moment to the people how much of that power they vest in a State government, and how much in the councils of the Union. . . . Our situation admits of a Union and our distresses point out its necessity. Our existence as a State depends on a strong and efficient Federal Government. The State has great natural advantages from its valuable and abundant staples, the situation of its principal seaport, from the command of the commerce of New Jersey by the river discharging in its bay, from the facility of intercourse with the Eastern States by the Sound, from the Hudson bearing on its bosom the wealth of the remote parts of the State. A lasting peace affords a prospect of its commanding the treasures of the West by the improvement of its internal navigation. The domestic debt of the Union is light; the back lands will pay the foreign debt, if a government vigorous enough to avail of that resource is adopted. For that Government, imports, at no distant day, will be sufficient, and taxation will only be needed for internal government. But the State has disadvantages, in the detached situation of its parts, particularly Staten Island and Long Island, in the vicinity of States which, in case of disunion, would be independent, and might be hostile. To the northeast, Vermont, a State with a brave and hardy people whom we have not the spirit to subdue nor the magnanimity to yield to, will avail of the weakness of New York. On the northwest there are the British posts and hostile savages. In case of domestic war, the Hudson, intersecting the State, weakens it by the difficulty of bringing one part to support the other. Consequently, our wealth and our weakness equally require the support of a Federal Union. A Union can only be found in the existing Confederation, or in that under consideration; and as a Union can only be founded upon the consent of the States, it should be sought when that consent may be expected. The powers of the Confederation were very similar to those in the proposed Constitution. Why had they not been efficient? Why was Vermont an independent State? Why have new States been rent from those in the West, in defiance of our plighted faith? Why are the British posts within the limits of the States? Because the Confederation is defective in principle and impeachable in execution, operating on States in their political capacity, not upon individuals. The powers intended to be vested in the Federal head have been impossible of execution, on the principle of a league of States totally separate and independent, therefore the form of government must be changed." Lansing said: "We ought to be extremely cautious how we establish a government which may give distinct interests to the rulers and the ruled. The objections urged against the Confederation are, that it affords no defense against foreign attack, and no security for domestic tranquillity. Both might be compassed if Congress could be vested with power to raise men and money, its legislation to act on individuals, after requisitions had been made and not complied with. This proposed Constitution I suppose to be a new experiment in politics. A Government so organized and possessing such powers will unavoidably terminate in depriving us of civil liberty. Conquest can do no more; that, in the present state of civilization, subjects us to be ruled by persons in whose appointment we have no agency. I am content to risk a possible, even a probable evil, to avoid a certain one. I contemplate the idea of disunion with pain, but, if it should ensue, what is to be apprehended? We are connected both by interest and affection with the Eastern States, we harbor no animosities against each other, we have no interfering territorial claims. Our manners are nearly similar, they are daily assimilating, and mutual advantages will probably prompt to mutual concessions and enable us to form a Union with them. I have declared that a consolidated government, even partaking in a great degree of republican principles, which had in its object the control of the inhabitants of the extensive territory of the United States, could not preserve the essential rights and liberties of the people. Reflection has given that belief greater force, and, as the representative of others, my duty is to offer amendments to this Constitution. Any amendment which will have a tendency to lessen the danger of the invasion of civil liberty by the General Government will meet my approbation, while none which in the remotest degree originate in local views will receive my concurrence." The Chancellor rejoined that, "if a Federal requisition upon a State was disregarded, subsequent Federal action upon individuals must be a source of eternal disorder, for then there would be a body of Federal officials acting in a State in direct opposition to the declared sense of its Legislature."

Melancthon Smith was "willing to sacrifice anything for a Union except the liberties of his country. That was the point to be debated. As for alarm from the inimical disposition of the Eastern States, he did not believe in the existence of such feelings. It could not be supposed that those States would war on us for exercising the rights of free men, deliberating and judging for ourselves on a subject the most interesting that ever came before any assembly. If war with our neighbors was to be the result of not acceding, debate was useless. We had better receive their dictates, if we were unable to resist them. The defects of the old Confederation needed as little proof as the necessity of a Union, but the question is not whether the old plan was bad, but whether the new one is good. To the clause before the committee his objections were threefold. To the apportionment—the principle of representation is that a free agent ought to be concerned in governing himself. Slaves have no will of their own, therefore the rule of apportionment was founded on an unjust principle, but if the result of accommodation, it must be admitted, utterly repugnant as it was. To the absence of a prohibition against a reduction of the number of the House—the first Congress would have the power to reduce the number, a power inconsistent with every principle of a free government. If the only security is the integrity of those trusted with power, it is idle to contend about constitutions. To the inadequacy of representation, twenty thousand should be entitled to a representative."

Hamilton rose: "The radical defect of the Confederation is that the laws of the Union apply only to the States in their corporate capacity. They can not be made effective but by an army. Can any reasonable man be well disposed toward a government which makes war and carnage the only means of supporting itself, a government that can only exist by the sword? What is the cure for this great evil? To enable the national laws to act upon individuals in the same manner as those of the State do. Why not, then, give that capacity to the Confederation? Because, though such a system may be safely intrusted with certain powers, to give it unlimited power over taxation and the national forces would be to establish a despotism; for, the definition of a despotism is, all power concentered in a single body." He then proceeded to disclose the reasonings and conclusions of the Federal Convention; to demonstrate that the project submitted was the outcome of a series of bargains; and to assert that if a convention of a similar character met again, met twenty times, or twenty thousand times, it must have the same difficulties to encounter, and the same clashing interests to reconcile. He also examined the equity of that bargain which apportioned representation. "Much has been said as to the impropriety of representing men who have no wills of their own. Whether this be reasoning or declamation, I will not presume to say. It is the unfortunate situation of the Southern States to have a great part of their population, as well as property, in blacks. The regulation complained of was one result of the spirit of accommodation which governed the Convention, and without this indulgence no union could have been formed. But, considering the peculiar advantages we derive from them, it is entirely just that they should be gratified. The Southern States have certain staples—tobacco, rice, indigo—which must be capital objects in treaties of commerce with foreign nations, and the advantages which they necessarily procure will be felt throughout all the States. But the justice of this plan will appear in another view. The best writers on government have held that representation should be compounded of persons and property. This rule has been adopted, as far as it could be, in the Constitution of New York. It will, however, be by no means admitted that the slaves are altogether property. They are men, though degraded to the condition of slavery. They are persons, known to the municipal laws of the States they inhabit, as well as to the laws of Nature. But representation and taxation ought to go together, and one uniform rule to apply to both. Would it be just to compute the slaves in the assessment of taxes, and discard them from the estimate in the apportionment of representation? Another circumstance ought to be considered. The rule is a general rule, and applies to all the States. You have a great number of people in your State who are not represented at all, and have no voice in your government. These will be included in the enumeration; not three fifths, but the whole. This proves that the advantages of the plan are not confined to the Southern States, but extend to other parts of the Union." As to the future number of representatives, he "admitted that there were no direct words of prohibition against a reduction, but the true and genuine construction of the clause does not give Congress power to reduce representation below the number as it stood." Upon the proper number to send a representative, he argued that "the proper number was a matter of opinion, between what all regarded as too small, and what all considered too great. The diversity in the State Legislatures proved it; but while one proportion might be more or less wise, no proportion, upon the basis assumed, could be unjust." More of an argument which surveyed the subject from every side need not be cited, except so much as replied to an objection of Melancthon Smith, who had contended for the smaller number, because "the larger would throw the office into the hands of the rich, and exclude the middling class, always the superior in virtue and patriotism." "The people have it in their power to elect the most meritorious men. While property continues to be pretty equally divided, and a considerable share of information pervades the community, the tendency of the people's suffrages will be to elevate merit, even from obscurity. As riches increase and accumulate in a few hands, as luxury prevails in society, virtue will, in a greater degree, be considered only a graceful appendage of wealth, and the tendency of things will be to depart from the republican standard. This is the real disposition of human nature; it is what neither the honorable member nor I can correct; it is a common misfortune that awaits our State Constitution as well as all others. But experience does not justify the supposition that there is more virtue in one class of men than in another. Look through the rich and the poor of a community, the learned and the unlearned. Where does virtue predominate? The difference, indeed, consists not in the quantity, but in the kind of vices which are incident to various classes. Here the advantage of character belongs to the wealthy; their vices are probably more favorable to the prosperity of the State than those of the indigent, and partake less of moral depravity." To a suggestion that the failure of the Confederation was largely due to the efforts of powerful and designing men, aiming at revolution and instigating disaffection, he answered: "The insinuation is false, the thing is impossible. I will venture to assert that no combination of designing men under heaven will be capable of making a government unpopular which in its principle is a wise and good one and vigorous in its operations."

At least one speech, and a very important one, of Hamilton's is not reported. Its purport can be guessed only from the answer of Smith: "The last speaker has assured the committee that the States would be checks upon the General Government, and had pledged himself to point out and demonstrate the operation of those checks. For himself, he could not see the possibility of checking a government of independent powers, which extended to all objects and measures without limitation. His own aim was to provide such checks as would not leave the exercise of government to the operation of causes which in their nature are variable and uncertain."

Mr. G. Livingston moved an amendment to the Senate clause that no person shall be a senator for more than six years in any twelve years, and that the Legislatures of the States may recall either or both, and elect others in their stead. Lansing supported it: "We are told that in one House, individuals, the people of the State, are represented, in the other its sovereignty. Should not the principal have the right to recall his agent? If the agent seeks his personal interest in disregard of that of the State, is the latter to be powerless for six years?" Smith suggested the additional possibility of corruption, both in the official and the people. He must have been asked, although the question does not appear, how corruption was practicable, and whence the fund for corruption. "More than one of the gentlemen have ridiculed my apprehensions of corruption. How, they say, are the people to be corrupted? By their own money. In many countries people pay their money to corrupt themselves, why should it not happen in this? I presume there is not a government in the world in which there is a greater scope for influence and corruption through the disposal of offices." Hamilton spoke twice against this amendment: "The zeal for liberty became predominant and excessive in us, as was natural, when the usurpation of Great Britain had to be met. That object is certainly very valuable, but there is another equally important—a principle of strength and stability in the organization of the Government and vigor in its operations; a purpose not to be accomplished but by the establishment of a select body founded particularly on this principle. It must be small, hold its authority during a considerable period, and have such an independence in the exercise of its powers as will divest it as much as possible of local prejudices. It should be so formed as to be the center of political knowledge, to pursue always a steady line of conduct, and to reduce every irregular propensity to system. Without this establishment, we may make experiments without end, but shall never have an efficient government. It is an unquestionable truth that the body of the people in every country sincerely desires its prosperity, but it is equally unquestionable that they do not possess the discernment and stability necessary for systematic government. To deny that they are frequently led into the grossest errors by misinformation and passion, would be a flattery their own good sense must despise. That branch of administration which involves our political relations with foreign states, a community will ever be incompetent to. These truths are not often held up in public assemblies, but they can not be unknown to any who hear me. Consider the purposes for which the Senate was instituted, and the nature of the business to be transacted. They, together with the President, are to manage all our concerns with foreign nations and understand all their interests and political systems. This knowledge is not soon acquired; but a small part is gained in the closet." The conclusion he deduced was, that the amendment assimilated the Senate to the House, and, just in proportion as the resemblance was closer, the mischief was greater. Up to this stage of the debate, the advocates of ratification had represented the Constitution as a system of checks and balances by which power and liberty were reconciled, checks and balances in the machinery of government, a check and balance between the Union and each of its constituent factors. Assertion of the latter was as constant as of the former. "The balance between the national and the State governments ought to be dwelt on with peculiar attention. It forms a double security for the people. If one encroaches on their rights, they will find a powerful protector in the other. Indeed, they will both be prevented from overpassing their constitutional limits by a certain rivalship which will ever subsist between them. The State governments possess inherent advantages, which will ever give them an influence and ascendency over the national Government, and will forever preclude the possibility of Federal encroachments." The ground upon which Hamilton predicted these assertions was: "There are certain social principles in human nature, from which we may draw the most solid conclusion with respect to the conduct of individuals and communities. We love our families more than our neighbors; we love our neighbors more than our countrymen in general. The human affections, like the solar heat, lose their intensity as they depart from the center, and become languid in proportion to the expansion of the circle in which they act. On these principles the attachment of the individual will be first and forever secured by the State governments, and they will be a mutual protection and support." The answers of Smith and Lansing were: "How, upon your theory, can a State government oppose the Federal Government, except by inciting its citizens to hostility? What remedy against misgovernment do you propose but rebellion? If the governments are rivals, must not one finally conquer and destroy the other? They ought not to be and need not be rivals; there should not be opposition, there should be harmony between them. The means are in our hands, the task is easy. What would be the functions of a government in an independent state are, in a union, divided between an organization created by a constitution, and an organization originally existing. The line between the powers of each ought to be so strongly marked and so obvious, that misconception will be impossible to a sane mind. How, otherwise, can right and wrong exist? Such a line is possible or impossible: if impossible, constitutional government is impossible, and the pretense of it hypocrisy; if possible, why not draw the line, or if you think it drawn, point it out?" The experience of daily life seems in some measure to support that view. A multitude of men can pass through a narrow street with ease and comfort if the ascending and descending streams of travel observe the law of the road. The subsequent speeches of Hamilton show the influence of this reasoning upon his mind: "In debates of this kind, it is extremely easy, on either side, to say a great number of plausible things. It is to be acknowledged that there is even a certain degree of truth in the reasonings on both sides. In this situation, it is the province of judgment and good sense to determine their force and application, and how far the arguments on one side are balanced by those on the other. The ingenious dress in which both may appear renders it a difficult task to make this decision, and the mind is frequently unable to come to a safe and solid conclusion. There are two objects in forming systems of government: safety for the people, and energy in the administration. When these objects are united, the certain tendency of the system will be the public welfare. If the latter object be neglected, the people's security will be as certainly sacrificed as by disregarding the former. Good constitutions are formed upon a comparison of the liberty of the individual, with the strength of the government. If the tone of either be too high, the other will be weakened too much. It is the happiest mode of conciliating these objects to institute one branch endowed with sensibility, and another with knowledge and firmness. Through the opposition and mutual control of these bodies the Government will reach in its operations the perfect balance between liberty and power." The validity of this argument rests upon the assumption that the two bodies represent distinct and hostile interests, and that each would be restrained from excess by the fear of a civil war, in which each could, with equal justice, claim to be defending the right. The subsequent admission that they were agencies of the same principals justified Smith and Lansing in denying such effect in the system, and therefore any force in the reasoning. He must be dull indeed who does not see that, in the absence of some check, a majority of the States, having a majority of population, can take possession of every branch of the Government and call and make their wills law, the other States occupying to them the relation which Great Britain claimed that the colonies occupied to her. The fact has been proved by experience, and the impotence of the judiciary as a check has also been proved by experience.

Driven from his claim of an internal check, Hamilton instantly changed front: "A Senator was an agent for the Union, not simply an agent for a State; the Senate should be formed so as to check in some measure the State governments; the interests of a State ought to be sacrificed for those of the Union." To the reply of Smith, "The interest of each State is the interest of every State, and must be so in a well-regulated government, why else was an equal vote given to each in the Senate?" his rejoinder was: "It has been remarked that there is an inconsistency in our admitting that the equal vote in the Senate was given to secure the rights of the States, and at the same time holding that their interests should be sacrificed to those of the Union. The committee can certainly perceive the difference between the rights of a State and its interests. The rights of a State are defined by the Constitution, and can not be invaded without a violation of it; but the interests of a State have no connection with the Constitution, and may in a thousand instances be constitutionally sacrificed." At this period Chancellor Livingston informed the committee "that the ninth State had ratified the Constitution, and that the Confederation was consequently dissolved. The question now before the committee was one of policy and expediency. He presumed the Convention would consider the situation of their country. Some might contemplate disunion without pain, and flatter themselves that some of the Southern States would form a league with us. He could not look without horror at the dangers to which any such confederacy would expose the State of New York. It might be political cowardice, but he had felt since yesterday an alteration of circumstances which had made a most solemn impression on his mind." Smith said "that the change of circumstances had not altered his feelings or his wishes on the subject; he had long been convinced that nine States would receive the Constitution."

Lansing said: "I do not agree that our particular circumstances are, in fact, altered since yesterday. That the ninth State has ratified the Constitution is an event which ought not to influence our deliberations. I presume that I shall not be charged with rashness if I continue to insist that it is still our duty to maintain our rights. Our dissent can not prevent the operation of the Government; since nine States have acceded to it, let them make the experiment. It has been said that some might contemplate disunion without terror. I have heard no sentiment from any gentleman that can warrant such an insinuation. We ought not, however, to suffer our fears to force us to adopt a system which is dangerous to liberty." Upon the several clauses of the Constitution, as the reading continued, amendments were offered and debates ensued. If not carrying conviction, they disclosed exactly how far men were apart, and who, on one or both sides, were anxious to find some basis of agreement. The opposite positions upon the scope of Federal power can be summed up on one side in the words of Hamilton, "When you have divided and nicely balanced the departments of government, when you have strongly connected the virtue of your rulers with their interest; when you have rendered your system as perfect as human forms can be, you must have confidence, you must give power"; and, on the other side, in the words of

Treadwell: "We are told that if government is properly organized, and the powers suitably distributed among the several members, it is unnecessary to provide any other security against the abuse of power; that power thus distributed needs not restriction. Is this a Whig principle? does not every Constitution on the continent contradict this position? Whatever be the design of the preachers, the tendency of their doctrines is clear—to corrupt our political faith, to take us off our guard, to lull to sleep that jealousy which, we are told by all writers, and is proved by all experience, to be essentially necessary for the preservation of freedom. In this Constitution we have departed widely from the principles and political faith of '76, when the spirit of liberty ran high and danger put a curb on ambition. Here we have no security for the rights of individuals, for the existence of our State governments, no Bill of Rights, no proper restriction of power. Our lives, our property, our consciences, are left wholly at the mercy of the Legislature; the powers of the judiciary may be extended to any degree short of Almighty. A union with our sister States I as ardently desire as any man, and that upon the most generous principles. The design of a union is safety. In one sense this may bring us to a state of safety; for it may reduce us to such a condition that we may be sure nothing worse can happen, and consequently have nothing to fear. This is a dreadful kind of safety, but it is the only kind of safety I can see in this union." Amendments and debates thereon (not recorded) occupied yet more than a fortnight; then Lansing moved a conditional ratification, with a Bill of Rights prefixed and amendments subjoined. The motion was carried. The vote is not given, but it was undoubtedly thirty to twenty-seven. Four days after, Mr. Jones moved that the words "in full confidence" be substituted in the form of ratification for the words "on condition." That motion was carried by thirty-one to twenty-nine. M. Smith, G. Livingston, and Williams, had passed over to their former adversaries. How they were won is not told, but may be easily guessed from the declaration by the Convention of a right of external check:

"The delegates of the people of the State of New York declare and make known that all power is originally vested in, and consequently derived from the people, and that government is instituted by them for their common interest, protection, and security; that the powers of government may be resumed by the people whenever it shall become necessary to their happiness; that every power, jurisdiction and right, which is not by the Constitution clearly delegated to the Congress of the United States or to the departments of government thereof, remains in the people of the several States or to their respective State governments to whom they may have granted the same; and that the clauses in said Constitution which declare that Congress shall not exercise certain powers do not imply that Congress is entitled to any powers not given by said Constitution, but such clauses are to be construed either as exceptions to certain specific powers, or inserted merely for greater caution." * The circular letter from the Convention to the Governors of the several States discloses more of the compromise which, in their view, justified the transfer of votes. A few sentences will exhibit it:

"Several articles in the Constitution appear so exceptionable to a majority of us, that nothing but the fullest confidence of obtaining a revision of them by a general convention, and an invincible reluctance to separate from our sister States, could have prevailed upon a sufficient number to ratify it, without stipulating for previous amendments. We all unite in the opinion that such a revision

* Rhode Island made the same claim of a right of external check in nearly the same words.

will be necessary to recommend it to the approbation and support of a numerous body of our constituents." The final vote was thirty to twenty-seven. Most of the counties were unanimously for, or against ratification. The trading-classes and the sea-washed counties were unanimous in their desire for the adoption of the Constitution; the agricultural class and the interior counties were the opponents. Before the final vote was taken, Lansing made a last effort to compel amendments. He moved a resolution that the State of New York reserve the right to withdraw from the Union after a certain number of years, unless the amendments proposed should previously be submitted to a general convention. That motion was negatived. The vote upon it is not in the printed report. The sense of the Convention on the subject of its long list of proposed amendments, is expressed in one paragraph of the circular letter: "Our amendments will manifest that none of them originated in local views; they are such as, if acceded to, must equally affect every State in the Union. Our attachment to our sister States, and the confidence we repose in them, can not be more forcibly demonstrated than by acceding to a government which many of us think very imperfect, and devolving the power of determining whether that government shall be rendered perpetual in its present form, or altered agreeably to our wishes, and a minority of the States with whom we unite." *

* The debates in the Convention of New York are like a Homeric battle, Hamilton against a host. His mind, "like an ample shield, took all their darts, with verge enough for more." The display of intellectual power is the more remarkable, from his total lack of faith in the plan. Of all men who have ever lived in the United States, his was the most complete mind. He seemed to absorb information. Upon any subject he could leap fully armed into the saddle, ready to meet all comers. If right, he was irresistible; if wrong, master of sophistry, he was almost irrefutable. His ideal of government was based upon human nature, as exhibited for thousands of years, not upon the then characteristics of American nature. He believed

that the existing passion for liberty must be evanescent, and that his countrymen would soon become as other men—more eager to rule, than jealous of rule. Instead of a Federal Union, he wished a legislative Union, with exceptions of power, and a Senate embodying the good features of the Senate of Rome; both it and the President to be elevated above party, by a tenure beyond party. He purposed that the democratic element should be fully represented in the House. His political career in the new Union was shaped by a belief, often expressed, that the Federal would be invaded by the State power, a consequence only to be averted by the gradual absorption of all the limitations upon Federal power. His theory of construction was inspired by a conviction that the federal principle must rest on force or on influence, not on good faith. No man, even believing that theory fatal, ever distrusted his motives or doubted his patriotism. To those, Burr, his sole rival in New York, did full justice, although a mutual personal enmity of long date was conjoined with political divergence. To those who with Gorham thought an hereditary monarchy the best of governments, there lacked an aristocracy, an insuperable objection, as he admitted; to those who thought with Hamilton, there lacked a plutocracy; to its creation, therefore, he addressed all his faculties.

THE NORTH CAROLINA CONVENTION, 1788.

When the Convention of North Carolina was organized, Galloway moved that the Constitution be discussed clause by clause.

Willie Jones moved that the question upon its adoption be immediately put. It had so long been the subject of the deliberation of every man that the members of the Convention were (he believed) prepared to vote.

Iredell was surprised at the motion: "A Constitution has been formed after much deliberation. It has had the sanction of men of the first characters, for their probity and understanding. It has also had the solemn ratification of ten States in the Union. It ought not to be adopted or rejected in a moment. Shall the representatives of North Carolina, assembled for the express purpose of deliberating upon the most important question that ever came before a people, refuse to discuss it, and discard reasoning as useless? I should not choose to determine on any question without mature reflection; and on this occasion my repugnance to a hasty decision is equal to the magnitude of the subject. I readily confess my present opinion strongly in its favor; but, notwithstanding, I have not come here resolved, at all events, to vote for its adoption. I have come to learn, and to judge. The Constitution ought to be discussed in such a manner that all possible light may be thrown on it. If they who think that it would be a bad government will unfold the reasons of their opinion, we may all concur in it. Can it be supposed that any here are so obstinate and tenacious of their opinion, that they will not recede upon reasons to change it? Has not every one here received useful knowledge from communication with others? Have not many of the members of this house, when members of the Assembly, frequently changed opinions upon subjects of legislation? If so, surely a subject of so complicated a nature, and which involves such serious consequences, requires the most ample discussion. I hope, therefore, that we shall imitate the laudable example of the other States, and go into a committee of the whole house, that the Constitution may be discussed clause by clause."

Jones, if members differed from him as to the propriety of his motion, submitted to their views.

Rev. Mr. Caldwell, in order to obviate the difficulty attending discussion, conceived it necessary to lay down certain fundamental principles of free government, compare the Constitution with them, and judge it by its consonance to them.

Davie observed that, to lay down a number of original principles would require a double investigation, the principles would have to be established, and then the comparison would have to be made.

Caldwell presented his principles: "A government is a compact between the rulers and the people. Such compact ought to be lawful in itself. It ought to be lawfully executed. Unalienable rights ought not to be given up, if not necessary. The compact ought to be mutual. It ought to be plain, obvious, and easily understood."

Iredell: "The first principle is erroneous. In other countries, where the origin of government is obscure, and its formation different from ours, government may be deemed a compact between the rulers and the people, with the consequence that, unless the rulers are guilty of oppression, the people, upon the principle of contract, which can not be annulled without the consent of both parties, have no right to new-model their government. Our government is founded upon much nobler principles. Our people are known with certainty to have originated it themselves. Those in power are their servants and agents, and the people, without their consent, may new-model their government whenever they think proper; not merely because it is oppressively exercised, but because they think another form will be more conducive to their welfare. It is upon the footing of this very principle that we are now met, to consider this Constitution before us."

Caldwell admitted that the government proposed did not resemble the European governments, but thought it yet partook of the nature of a compact.

Maclaine said the "principles" were taken from sources which can not hold here. In England the government is a compact between the people and the king.

Goudry thought that there was a quibble upon words. Compact, agreement, covenant, bargain, or what not, the intent of the instrument was a concession of power by the people to rulers. We know private interest generally governs mankind. Power belongs originally to the people, but, if rulers are not well guarded, that power may be usurped from them; hence, the necessity of general rules.

Iredell said: "The line between power which is given, and which is retained, ought to be as accurately drawn as possible. In this system, the line is most accurately drawn, by the positive grant of powers to the General Government. But a compact between the rulers and the ruled is certainly not the principle of this government. Will any man say that, if there be a compact, it can be altered without the consent of both parties? Those who govern, unless they grossly abuse their trust, which is held an implied violation of the compact, and therefore a dissolution of it, have a right to say that they do not choose that the government should be changed. But have any of the officers of our government a right to say so, if the people choose to change it? Surely not."

Spencer: "I conceive that it will retard business to consider the proposal. It does not apply to the present circumstances. When there is a king, or other governors, there is a compact between the people and him. In this case, in regard to the government it is proposed to adopt, there is no ruler or governor."

The previous question, being put, was carried by an immense majority; then the motion to consider the Constitution, clause by clause, was debated and carried by a great majority.

Caldwell inquired the meaning of "We, the people."

Davie supposed the question to be prompted by the assumption that the Federal Convention had exceeded its powers; as a member of that Convention, he could answer for its action. Its mission was "to decide upon the most effectual means of removing the defects of our Federal Union. That was a general discretionary authority, to propose any alteration thought necessary and proper. The State Legislatures were afterward to review the proceedings. Through their recommendation the plan is submitted to the people, and it must remain a dead letter, or receive its operation from the fiat of this Convention. The general objects of the Union are to protect us against foreign invasion, internal commotions and insurrections, and to promote the commerce, agriculture, and manufactures of America. To neither was the Confederation competent; and, as it would have been dangerous to lodge additional power in a single body, a different organization was necessary. To form some balance, the departments of government were separated, and the Legislature divided into two branches. The House is immediately elected by the people, the Senate represents the sovereignty of the States. The difference of the States, in point of importance and magnitude, was an additional reason for the two branches. The protection of the small States, against the ambition and influence of the larger, could only be effected by arming them with equal power in one branch of the Legislature. Without that check, the consent of the smaller States could not have been obtained. The executive is separated in its functions from the legislative as well as the nature of things would admit. A radical defect of the old system was, that it legislated for States, not individuals, and that its powers could only be executed by military force, instead of by the intervention of the civil magistrate. Every one acquainted with the relative situation of the States, and the genius of our citizens, must acknowledge that, if the government was to be carried on by military force, the citizens of America would be rendered the most implacable enemies to one another; and, if it could be thus carried into effect against the small States, it could not be put in force against the larger and more powerful. The Convention knew that all governments, merely federal, had been short-lived, or had existed from principles extraneous to their constitution, or from external causes, which had no dependence on the nature of their governments; therefore it departed from that solecism in politics, the principle of legislation for States, in their political capacity. The great extent of country appeared a formidable difficulty, but a confederate government appears, at least in theory, capable of embracing the various interests of the most extensive territory. There was a real difficulty in conciliating a number of jarring interests, arising from the incidental, but unalterable, difference between the States, in point of territory, situation, climate, and rivalship in commerce. Each, therefore, amicably and wisely relinquished its particular views. I hope that the same spirit of amity, of mutual deference, and concession, to which the Federal Convention attributed the Constitution, will govern the deliberation and decision of this Convention."

Taylor returned to "We, the people." He saw in these words an intention of consolidation. Maclaine was astonished to hear objections to the preamble: "Is not this a dispute about words, without any meaning whatever? This Constitution is a blank until it is adopted by the people. When that is done here, is it not the people of North Carolina that do it, joined with the people of the other States that have adopted it? The expression, then, is right."

Caldwell remarked that, while all legislative power was placed in the Congress, the Vice-President was associated with the legislative power by his casting vote.

Davie stated why the Federal Convention imposed that duty on the Vice-President. "The commercial jealousy between the Eastern and Southern States had a principal share in this business. It might happen, in important cases, that the voices would be equally divided. Indecision might be inconvenient, and dangerous to the public. The Vice-President, in consequence of his election, is the creature of no particular State or district. He must possess the confidence of the States in a very great degree, and is consequently the most proper person to decide on cases of that kind. It is impossible that any officer could be chosen more impartially." Maclaine added that a provision of the sort was to be found in all legislative bodies, was useful, expedient, and calculated to prevent the operation of the government from being impeded.

Lenoir observed that the President was also connected, to some extent, with the legislative powers; whereupon Iredell attempted a distinction between the power to legislate and the power to prevent legislation. There are no two provisions in the Constitution more wise than the casting vote of the Vice-President and the veto of the President, and none more defensible; but to contend that the power which enables something to become, or forbids it to become law, is not a legislative power, is to juggle with words. The impolicy of not meeting an issue squarely, was demonstrated on the next objection; that the executive was blended with the legislative power, as the Senate acted upon treaties. The answer might have been: This is a government *sui generis*. There is in it an association, to some extent, of the legislative and executive functions, very prudent and proper. There is an agency for making statutes, and an agency for making treaties; the functions are different, if the persons are the same. Instead of which, a verbal distinction was drawn, which did not satisfy inquiry, and increased suspicion. Upon the word "sole," in the clause which gives to the House of Representatives the power of impeachments, debate was sharp. No one contended that the word was not superfluous, although it was claimed that the surplusage could not injure, as by the context it was plain that impeachment was limited to officers of the United States. The answer in substance was: Every unnecessary word in a Constitution is dangerous; casuistry can find exercise enough in the imperfection of language, without extraneous aid. "Sole" may contain danger. Upon the Federal regulation of the time, place, and manner of elections, Governor Johnston was forced to say: "Although a great admirer of the Constitution, I can not comprehend the reason of this part. This power in Congress appears useless, so long as the State Legislatures have the power not to choose senators; but I do not consider this blemish in the Constitution sufficient for rejection. I observe that every State, which has adopted and recommended alterations, has given directions to remove this objection."

Spencer, conscious as he was of the excellences of the

Constitution, and reluctant to find fault, could not consent to a provision which sapped the foundations of those governments on which the happiness of the States and of the General Government must depend. Iredell appealed to the candor and moderation of the last speaker to consider the language in connection with the rest of the instrument. "Representatives were to be chosen every two years; they must be chosen. Whether in January, March, or any other month, was all that was left for future congressional regulation. He could see in the possibilities of a State Legislature being unable to act in case of war, or in the combination of some great States not to send representatives, the reasons which prompted the clause."

He was careful not to touch upon "place and manner." Spencer responded: "I only meant to say that the words are exceedingly vague. They may admit of the construction just given; they may admit of a contrary construction. In a matter of so great moment, words ought not to be so vague and indeterminate. No man wishes for a Federal Government more than I do. I consider it necessary to our happiness; but at the same time when we form a government which must entail happiness or misery on posterity, nothing is of more consequence than settling it so as to exclude animosity, and a contest between the Federal and the individual governments. The words under consideration are words of very great extent, and so vague and uncertain that they must ultimately destroy the whole liberty of the United States."

Davie asserted two reasons for the existence of the clause. If he was justified by facts, they must be part of an unwritten history of the Federal Convention. The principal reason was to prevent the dissolution of the Government by designing States. Without this control in Congress, the large States might successfully combine to destroy the Federal Government. Another principal reason was, that it would operate in favor of the people, against the ambitious designs of the Federal Senate. He next inquired as to the effect of the clause. A fundamental principle beyond the reach of the General or State government is, that representatives shall be chosen every two years; that the qualifications of these electors shall be the qualifications of electors to the most numerous branch of the State Legislature, and that senators shall be chosen for six years. All the power of the State Legislature is to regulate the when, the where, and the how; that was equally the power of Congress—no less, no more.

Bloodworth said: "It was easy to mention that the control of Congress should be exerted when a State neglected, refused, or was unable, in case of invasion, to regulate elections. If that was the meaning, why was it not expressed? If more was meant, that was a sufficient reason to reject the Constitution. There seemed to be a strange inconsistency in the arguments adduced."

Spencer, willing to give the General Government impost, excise, and direct taxation, in case of war, was unwilling to concede the latter power during peace, until requisitions had been made, neglected, or refused. The power of direct taxation should be kept as near to the people as possible.

Whitmill Hill remarked that while the general wish was to empower Congress to raise all necessary sums, there was a great difference of opinion as to the better mode. Two circumstances might weigh with the committee: First, that the people of North Carolina had the honesty and the ability to pay any reasonable tax; secondly, that when it was once known to foreign nations that the Government and its finances were upon a respectable basis, money for any emergency could be borrowed on advantageous terms.

Governor Johnston denied the assumption that, under the proposed system, the power of taxation was taken out of the hands of the people: "Taxes must be voted by their representatives. If there were danger from that source, where can political security be found? It is said that our proportion of representation is small; then our proportion of taxation is small; and, unless we suppose that all the members of Congress will combine to ruin their constituents, there can be no reason for fear."

Goudry and McDowell disclosed the reasons for the overwhelming opposition to the grant of power of direct taxation: "Some represent us as honest, but not rich; others as rich, but not honest. The fact is, we are very poor, and not able to bear taxation for more than one government. If there are two, with equal right to tax, one must give way. The tendency of the Constitution to destroy the State governments must be clear to every man of common understanding."

Other clauses were read without debate, until that which admitted the slave-trade was reached.

McDowell asked the reasons of the Federal Convention for that exception.

Spraight answered that it was the result of a compromise between the Eastern and the Southern States. South Carolina and Georgia had lost a great many slaves during the war, and wished to supply the loss. As North Carolina had not passed any law to prohibit the importation of negroes, her delegates had not felt authorized to contend for an immediate prohibition of it.

By both sides the utmost repugnance was manifested to the clause. The Convention only yielded its detestation, to the reasoning of Iredell, that the Constitution really presented the only means, so far as Americans were concerned, of terminating an odious traffic. On the subject of slavery itself, the sentiment of North Carolina and Virginia appears to have been identical. Two difficulties stood in the way of manumission: a right of property, which had been universally recognized up to that period, and a repugnance of race. Perhaps both were never more clearly and calmly stated than in this discussion, by Galloway. After expressing his horror of an "abominable traffic," he continued: "With respect to the abolition of slavery, it requires the utmost consideration. The property of the Southern States is principally in slaves; if slavery is done away with, this property will be destroyed. If we must manumit our slaves, to what country shall we send them? It is impossible for us to be happy, if, after manumission, they are to stay among us." The aversion of race is to some extent cruel, and to some extent silly, but it is not a mere prejudice; it has some reason in the nature of things.

The clause which vested executive power having been read, and no observation made, Davie expressed "surprise at the silence and gloomy jealousy of the opposition. Out-of-doors, no feature of the Constitution had met with such violent, indeed, virulent censure."

Taylor thought that, even if the Convention possessed the power to amend the Constitution, every part need not be discussed, as some were not objectionable; his objection was to the power of Congress to determine the time of choosing the electors and the day on which they should give their votes. His meaning, in the objection "that everything which could be, should be, definitely fixed, beyond the future passions of men," was mistaken for concern as to a detail, not as to a principle.

The answers, with justice, sustained the detail, but did not touch the scruple. Upon the association of the Senate with the President, in treaty-making and appointment to office, Spencer detailed the grounds of opposition, which, if neither accepted nor acceptable, were based upon a careful study of political science: "It is an essential article in our Constitution that the executive, the legislative, and the supreme judicial powers of government ought to be forever separate and distinct from each other. The Senate, in the proposed plan, are possessed of legislative power in conjunction with the House. They are possessed of the sole power of trying impeachments, and by this clause, in effect, they possess the chief executive power. They form treaties which are to be the law of the land. They control the appointment, practically, of all the officers of the United States. The President may nominate, but they have a negative upon his nomination. He will be obliged, finally, to acquiesce in the appointment of those whom in reality the Senate will nominate, or else no appointment will be made. Hence, it is easy to perceive that the President, in order to do any business, or to answer any purpose in this department of his office, and to keep himself out of perpetual hot water, will be under a necessity to form a connection with that powerful body, and be contented to put himself at the head of the leading members who compose it. I do not expect, at this day, that the outline and organization of the proposed government will be materially changed, but it would have been infinitely better, and more secure, if the President had been provided with a Standing Council, composed of a member from each State, whose term of office might have been the same as his own. Two very important consequences would result, which can not result from the present plan. The first, that the executive department, being separate and distinct, the President and his Council, any or either, would be amenable to the justice of the land. As it is, I do not conceive that the President can even be tried by the Senate, with any effect, or to any purpose, for any misdemeanor in office, unless it should extend to high treason, or unless they should wish to fix the odium of any measure upon him, in order to exculpate themselves. The other important consequence is, that the President would have an independence which he does not have in this plan. If no other argument for a council could be urged, the diminution of the power of the Senate would be sufficient." Davie admitted "that a total separation of the branches of government was desirable, but it has never been found entirely practicable. So far as it was departed from in this system, the causes would be found in the extreme jealousy of executive power in the American mind, and the difference in size, wealth, and population of the States. The smaller States had a disproportionate influence in the government, which they insisted was necessary to their safety. That influence is exerted in the Senate. The difficulty could not be got over. It arose from the unalterable nature of things. Upon some subjects the smaller States would not agree that the House should have a voice, and upon the same subject none of the States would agree that the President should have an exclusive voice. Not only the present distribution of power is good in itself, but no one can suggest a better. A council would be open to every objection that can be urged against the Senate, and to other objections which can not be urged against the Senate. The Senate represents the Federal principle of the government and is the safeguard against consolidation. Its great power is commensurate with its functions." Iredell added: "God forbid that in any country a man should be punished for want of judgment! For errors of the heart, should any be committed here, there is a ready way to punishment. That is a responsibility which answers every purpose a people jealous of their liberties can ask. Parties must exist, and may be bitter; the malignity of party will interpret difference of opinion, as deliberate wickedness."

Upon the judiciary clause, debate was not conducive to harmony. Davie urged the undeniable political truth that the judicial must be coextensive with the legislative power. The proposition was not denied; the contention turned upon the point whether the judicial was not, or might not, become more extensive, and the Constitution become judge-made, not convention-made. The object of a Constitution being to fix the *meum* and *tuum* between the States, and between the General Government and the States, the judiciary, it was conceded, might be qualified and trusted to decide whether either was invaded, but not to determine whether the *meum* and *tuum* had been properly partitioned. This course of reasoning led, naturally, to the consideration of the necessity for a Bill of Rights. Davie and others insisted that, though necessary in a monarchy, it was unnecessary in such a government, the Constitution itself being a Bill of Rights, as it excluded whatever was not included.

Spencer answered: "It is said that what is not given up to the United States will be retained by the individual States. I know it ought to be so, and should be understood so, but it is not declared, as it was in the Confederation. What is not declared is apt to be overlooked. The language in the Articles of Confederation was the equivalent of a Bill of Rights."

Iredell asked "what more could be necessary when the people declare how much they give. The Constitution may be considered as a great power of attorney. If we had formed a general Legislature, with undefined powers, a Bill of Rights would have been not only proper, but necessary, to operate exceptions to the legislative authority." Spencer's belief that what is generally understood ought to be distinctly stated, seems to be approved by events. Had the friends of the Constitution embodied in it, or in an amendment, the declarations they made in conventions, the epithets of their posterity might have been differently distributed. The omission of mention of a jury in civil cases, while specified in criminal cases, excited great alarm.

Iredell stated the cause of the omission: "Let any

gentleman consider the difficulties in which the Federal Convention was placed. A Union was absolutely necessary. Everything could be agreed upon except the regulation of the trial by jury in civil cases. All were anxious to establish it on the best footing, but found that they could fix upon no permanent rule that was not liable to great objections and difficulties. If the delegates could not agree among themselves, they had still less reason to believe that all the States would have unanimously agreed to any one plan that could be proposed. They therefore thought it better to leave the regulations to the Legislature. It has been said that the objection might have been obviated by the addition of five or six lines. If, by the addition of five or six hundred lines, this invaluable object could have been secured, I should have thought the Convention criminal in omitting it."

Among the amendments to the Constitution, a few lines dissipated doubts and dispelled fears upon that point.

Iredell explained the reasons for the "fugitive-slave" clause: "Some of the Northern States have emancipated their slaves. If any of our slaves go there, and remain a certain time, they would, under present laws, be entitled to their freedom, so that their masters could not get them again, to prevent which this clause is inserted." The reasons for the prohibition to the States, of issuing paper money, and making anything, save gold and silver, a legal tender, were asked of those members who had been delegates to the Federal Convention. The answer was: "Mischief had been done, it could not be repaired, but some limitations to that great political evil had to be formed. The people of Massachusetts and Connecticut had been great sufferers by the dishonesty of Rhode Island, and similar complaints existed against this State. The clause became, in some measure, a preliminary, with the delegates who represented the other States. 'You have,' said they, 'by your iniquitous laws, and paper emissions, shamefully defrauded our citizens. The Confederation prevented our compelling you to do them justice; but, before we confederate with you again, you must not only agree to be honest, but put it out of your power to be dishonest.'"

Galloway asked if the inhibition on a State to pass a law impairing the obligation of contracts applied to the public securities of a State. Davie answered: "In no part of the Constitution is power vested to interfere with the public securities of a State. The clause refers to contracts between individuals."

Abbot wished to know, as treaties were to become the supreme law of the land, whether a treaty could engage to some particular religion, and also, as no religious test was required, whether, in the oath to support the Constitution, Juno, Minerva, or Pluto, might not be the deities invoked.

Iredell answered, "The question has also been asked whether the Pope may not be elected President." With polite circumlocution, he suggested that the assumption of sanity, as the normal condition of mankind, was the only possible answer to some questions. "The absence of any religious test was the glory of the Constitution. Men are left to believe as they can; admit the least difference, and the door is opened to persecution. Whatever form binds the conscience, is the essence of an oath." Abbot further asked the import of the guarantee of a republican form of government.

Iredell replied, "With thirteen States, confederated upon a republican principle, it was essential to the harmony and existence of the Confederacy, that each should have a republican government, and that no one should have a right to establish a monarchy or an aristocracy."

The reading of the Constitution finished, the question next in order was, What will be the relation of North

Carolina to the other States, if she refuses to adopt? "She will be a foreign State," said Davie, "and can communicate with the United States only through embassadors." "What then," it was asked, "becomes of the faith plighted by the Articles of Confederation? If some States can absolve themselves at will from the obligations of those, why not from the obligations of the Constitution." . In the Federal Convention the same inquiry had been made: "If nine States can withdraw from thirteen, why not six from nine, four from six?" Answer was avoided there, but not in the Convention of North Carolina.

"The great principle," said Iredell, "the fundamental principle upon which our government is founded, is the safety of the people. For their welfare government is instituted, and this ought to be its object, whatever its form. Our governments have clearly been created by the people themselves; the same authority that created can destroy, and the people may undoubtedly change the government, not because it is ill-exercised, but because they conceive that another form will be more conducive to their welfare. It is suggested that, though ten States have adopted the Constitution, they had no right to dissolve the old Confederation, that the Articles still subsist, and the old Union remains, of which we are a part. That this is true may well be doubted. All writers agree that, if the principles of a Constitution are violated, the Constitution itself is dissolved, or may be, at the pleasure of the parties to it. The principles of the Confederation have not seldom been violated, and North Carolina, as well as others, has been an offender. This Constitution is proposed to the thirteen States. The desire was, that all should agree; but, if not, care was taken that at least nine might save themselves from destruction."

Davie took other ground: "It is said that it is a rule

of law that the same solemnities are necessary to annul as were necessary to create or establish a compact; and that, as thirteen States created, so thirteen States must concur in the dissolution of the Confederacy. This may be the talk of a lawyer or a judge, but is not the talk of a politician. Every man of common sense knows that political power is political right. In every republican community, whether confederated or separate, a majority binds the minority.* The voice of the majority of the people of America gave the Confederation validity; the same authority can and will annul it. Adoption places us in the Union; rejection extinguishes the right."

If Iredell was right, the claimants under the Articles of Confederation had no cause of complaint; if Davie was right, it made no difference if they had, and therefore both, with Johnston, urged adoption by arguments which reason could not answer. "You will, you admit, be satisfied with this Constitution if amended; adopt, and your strength, added to that of those States, eager for the same amendments, can carry them; reject, and your weakness will count against you, in place of your strength counting for you. Adopt, and you can help shape the new government and share in the feast; reject now, and when you adopt, as you eventually must, you will have to accept the shaping of others, and find only the crumbs."

Upon the motion to ratify, the yeas were 84, and the

---

* Pennsylvania is an illustration. The charter of that colony reserved to Great Britain the right of taxation. Her claims to independence could not, therefore, have been based upon an invasion of charter liberties, that usurpation of an unwarranted jurisdiction denounced by the other colonies, but must have rested upon an inherent right in one community, upon its judgment of the necessity to renounce a political connection with another. Two speeches of great ability, made in her Convention, in advocacy of ratification of the Constitution, exist, though other record of debate is lost. Neither recognizes any obligation of faith under the Articles of Confederation, and they differ as to the character and effect of the instrument they recommend.

nays 184. Upon the motion neither to adopt nor reject, the yeas were 184, and the nays 84. By the same vote any impost passed by the United States was recommended to be passed by the Legislature of North Carolina, the proceeds to be held at the disposition of Congress.

The motive of the majority, if surmise be permissible, was to serve the desire for amendments, the difference of opinion between the majority and minority being as to whether such service would be more efficient by presence in, or absence from, the councils of the new Union.

At the first session of Congress, held in the city of New York, 4th of March, 1789, twelve amendments were proposed to the Legislatures of the States, of which ten were adopted. On the 11th of January, 1790, the President communicated to both Houses of Congress the ratification of the Constitution by North Carolina.

THE SOUTH CAROLINA CONVENTION, 1788.

The debates in the Convention of South Carolina are said to have been distinguished by the ability with which ratification was advocated and opposed, but no report of them is extant. A fragment remains; from that, from the vote upon the question, and from the debate in the Legislature, upon the motion for the call of a convention, some knowledge may be acquired of those who favored and those who opposed the adoption of the Constitution, and some conception of the reasoning upon which their action was based. What, in later years, was termed "the slave power," the professions, and the commercial class, as a general rule, were passionate adorers of the Constitution; the yeomanry of the upper parishes were obdurate skeptics. As in other States, favor and disfavor seem to have been largely local.

In the House of Representatives of the State of South Carolina, upon the motion for the call of a State Convention, after the Constitution had been read, Charles Pinckney, a delegate to the Federal Convention, opened the debate, by enumerating the causes which led to that Convention, and by stating that, when it met, the first question in the view of almost every member was, "Shall the old plan be amended, or a new one devised?" "Conscious that the Confederation, though possessing the outlines of a good government, was, strictly speaking, a league destitute of the elements of permanency and coercive operation, the Convention felt the necessity of establishing a government which, instead of requiring the intervention of thirteen Legislatures between demand and compliance, operated upon the people in the first instance. Upon that point the members did not differ, however much they differed upon the question of power. Upon the distribution of influence, in a system possessing extensive national authorities, the compromise between the larger and the smaller States, though originally opposed by him, seemed far from injudicious. The judiciary, under wise management, would be the key-stone of the arch, for in peace more depended upon the integrity and energy of the judiciary than upon any other branch of the government. The Executive was not constructed upon a principle as firm and permanent as he could wish, but as much so as the genius and temper of the people would permit. As commander-in-chief of the land and naval forces, he could neither raise nor support them by his authority, and his negative upon laws could be overridden. He could not make a treaty, nor appoint to office, without the concurrence of a Senate, in which the States had each an equal voice. In a Union so extensive as this would be, composed of so many State governments, inhabited by a people characterized, as our citizens are, by an impatience of any act which looks like an infringement of their rights, an invasion of them by the Federal head appeared the most remote of all public dangers. To what limits a republic of States may extend, how far it may be capable of uniting the liberty of a small commonwealth with the safety of a peaceful empire, whether among the co-ordinate powers dissensions and jealousies may not arise, which, for the want of a common superior, will proceed to fatal extremities, were questions upon which the example of any nation did not authorize decision. It was an experiment admittedly, but an experiment which could be made upon a scale so extensive, and under circumstances so promising, as to be the fairest in favor of human nature, and its firm establishment better calculated to answer the great ends of public happiness than any ever yet devised." In his address to the Convention, Pinckney gave wider scope to his reasoning: "The first knowledge necessary to be acquired is that of a people for whom a system is to be formed, for, unless acquainted with their situation, their habits, opinions, and resources, it would be impossible to frame a government upon adequate or practicable principles. None of the distinctions of rank which exist in Europe do, or, in all probability, ever will, exist in the Union. The only distinction which may take place is that of wealth. Riches, no doubt, will have their influence; and, when suffered to increase to large amounts in a few hands, may become dangerous, particularly when, from the cheapness of labor and the scarcity of money, a great proportion of the people are poor. That danger is very little to be apprehended for two reasons—the destruction of the right of primogeniture, and the nearly equal division of landed property in the Eastern and Northern States. Few have large, and few have not small tracts. The greater part of the people are employed in cultivating their own lands, the rest in handicraft and commerce. Plain tables, clothing, and furniture prevail in their houses, and expensive appearances are avoided. Among the landed interest few are rich, and few are very poor, nor, while the States are capable of supporting so many more inhabitants than they contain at present, while so vast a territory on our frontier remains uncultivated and unexplored, while the means of subsistence are so much within every man's power, are those dangerous distinctions of fortune, prevalent in other countries, to be expected. The people of the Union may be classed as follows: Commercial men, who will be of consequence, or not, in the political scale, as commerce may be an object of the attention of the Government. Presuming that proper sentiments upon that subject will ultimately prevail, it does not appear that the commercial line will ever have much influence in the politics of the Union. Foreign trade is one of those enemies to be extremely guarded against, more so than any other, as none will have a more unfavorable operation; it is the root of the present distress, the source from which future national calamities will grow, unless great care is taken to prevent it. Divided as we are from the Old World, we should have nothing to do with its politics, and as little as possible with its commerce; it can never improve, but must inevitably corrupt us. Another class is that of professional men, who, from their education and pursuits, must and will have considerable influence, while government retains the republican principle, and its affairs are regulated in assemblies of the people. The third class, with which may be connected the mechanical interest, is the landed interest; the owners and cultivators of the soil, the men attached to the truest interest of their country, from those motives that always bind and secure the affections of a nation. Here rests, and it is to be hoped will always continue to rest, all the authority of the Government. Fortunately for their harmony, these classes are connected with and dependent on each other; from which mutual dependence, mediocrity of fortune is the leading feature in our national character. Another distinguishing feature of the Union is its division into individual States, differing in extent of territory, manners, products, and population. Those acquainted with the Eastern States, the reasons of their migration, and their pursuits, habits, and principles, know that they are essentially different from those of the Middle and Southern States; that they retain all those opinions respecting government and religion which first induced their ancestors to cross the Atlantic; and that they are perhaps more purely republican in habits and sentiments than any other part of the Union. The inhabitants of New York, and the eastern part of New Jersey, originally Dutch settlements, seem to have altered less than might have been expected in the course of a century; indeed, the greater part of New York may still be considered a Dutch settlement, the people in the interior generally using the Dutch language in their families, and having little varied from their ancient customs. Pennsylvania and Delaware are nearly one half inhabited by Quakers, whose passive principles upon the governmental questions, and rigid opinions upon the personal, render them extremely different from the citizens of the Eastern and Southern States. Maryland was originally a Roman Catholic colony; a great number of its inhabitants, among whom some of the most wealthy and cultivated, still profess that faith. A striking difference must always exist between the Independents of the East, the Calvinists and Quakers of the Middle States, and the Roman Catholics of Maryland; but that is not to be compared with the difference between the inhabitants of the Northern and Southern States; by Southern and Northern, meaning Maryland and the States south of her, and, by Northern, the others. Nature has drawn as strong marks of distinction in the habits and manners of the people as in their climates and productions. The Southern citizen beholds, with a kind of surprise, the simple manners of the East, and is often induced to entertain undeserved opinions of the apparent purity of the Quakers; while they, in turn, seem concerned at what they term the extravagance and dissipation of their Southern brethren, and reprobate, as an unpardonable moral and political evil, the dominion held over a part of the human race." Premising that systems and laws have a powerful effect upon manners, and that all the States had adhered to the republican principle, though differing as to the best mode of preserving it, he passed in review the Constitutions of the several States, giving the palm to New York. Turning to antiquity, he claimed that from its history instruction could not be drawn, because little of it was accurately known, and that little showed that representation, the fundamental of a republic, had not been practiced. In the modern world there had been, in no sense of the word, a confederated republic; and he analyzed the systems which bore some resemblance to the one proposed, and distinguished their non-conformity. He then examined the three simple systems of government—monarchy, oligarchy, and democracy—exhibited their advantages and disadvantages, and claimed that the Constitution embodied all the good, and eliminated all the bad, of each. Moreover, if a republic did not exclude dissensions and tumults, they must be less dangerous in large confederated states than in small societies.

To return to the debate in the Legislature. Judge Pendleton said that "ministers in England might be impeached for advising illegal measures. How could the Senate be punished, before what tribunal arraigned, and if the President were impeached for making a bad treaty, must he not be sheltered by the consent of the Senate?" General C. C. Pinckney answered: "That question unveils one of the geatest difficulties in framing the Constitution. The treaty-making power must be placed somewhere, and might be placed in three depositories; to each there were objections, therefore the least liable to objection was selected. As the Senate was not a permanent body, senators might be tried by succeeding senators." Mr. Lowndes suggested that "as treaties became the law of the land, the President and two thirds of the Senate were absolute." Mr. Pringle interposed a distinction between the power to make law through treaties and a general legislative power. Mr. Lowndes continued: "If this Constitution is adopted, the sun of the Southern States will set, never to rise. Exclusive of Rhode Island, six of the Eastern States formed a majority in the House. Is it consonant with reason, with wisdom, or with policy, to suppose that, in a Legislature where a majority has different interests from a minority, the minority has the smallest chance of gaining adequate advantages? Our delegates, undoubtedly, did all in their power to procure a proportionate share in this new government, but the little they had gained proved what may be expected in the future. The interest of the Northern States will so predominate as to divest this State of any pretensions to the title of a republic. What cause was there of jealousy for the importation of negroes? That trade can be justified on the principles of religion, humanity, and justice; for to translate a set of human beings from a bad country to a better was fulfilling every part of those principles." Mr. Rutledge answered: "We have our full share of the House; fears of the Northern interest, at all times prevailing, are unfounded, for several of the Northern States are already full of people, and the migrations to the South are great. We shall, in a few years, rise high in our representation, while their States will keep their present position."

General Pinckney, in answer to Mr. Lowndes, who had reiterated that all the advantages which captivated gentlemen were small in proportion to the evils to be apprehended from a majority, governed by ideas and prejudices differing extremely from theirs, spoke more fully: "Every member who attended the Convention was, from the beginning, sensible of the necessity of giving greater powers to the Federal Government. As we found it necessary to give it very extensive powers over the persons and estates of citizens, we thought it right to draw one branch of the Legislature immediately from the people, and that both wealth and numbers should be considered in representation. We were at a loss for some time for a rule to ascertain the proportionate wealth of the States. At last we thought that the productive labor of the inhabitants was the best rule. In conformity to this rule, joined to a spirit of concession, we determined that representatives should be apportioned among the several States, by adding to the whole number of free persons three fifths of the slaves. We thus obtained a representation for our property, and I did not expect we conceded too much to the Eastern States, when they allowed us a representation for a species of property which they have not among them. The numbers in the different States, according to the most accurate accounts we could obtain, were:

New Hampshire	102,000
Massachusetts	360,000
Rhode Island	58,000
Connecticut	202,000
New York	233,000
New Jersey	130,000
Pennsylvania	360,000
Delaware	37,000
Maryland, including $\frac{3}{5}$ 80,000 negroes	218,000
Virginia, including $\frac{3}{5}$ 280,000 negroes	420,000
North Carolina, including $\frac{3}{5}$ 60,000 negroes	200,000
South Carolina, including $\frac{3}{5}$ 80,000 negroes	150,000
Georgia, including $\frac{3}{5}$ 20,000 negroes	90,000

South Carolina has one thirteenth of the representatives, all she is entitled to, and all she has in the Confederation. As the Eastern States are full of people, and the migration is south and southwestwardly, it is not probable that the representation of the South will be inadequate. The Southern States have been termed the weak States; they are so weak that they could not form a Union by themselves, that would effectually protect them. Without a Union with the other States, South Carolina would soon fall. Is any one such a Quixote as to suppose that this State could maintain her independence alone, or in connection with the other Southern States? Let an invading power send a naval force into the Chesapeake, to keep Virginia in alarm, and attack South Carolina, with such a naval and military force as Sir Henry Clinton brought here in 1780, and, though they might not soon conquer us, they would certainly do us infinite mischief, and, if they considerably increased their numbers, we should probably fall. From the nature of our climate, and the fewness of our inhabitants, undoubtedly the weaker, should we not endeavor to form a close union with the Eastern States, which are strong? Ought we not to endeavor to increase that species of strength which will render them of most service to us in peace and in war, their navy? By doing this, we render it their particular interest to afford us every assistance in their power, as every wound we receive will eventually affect them. Their country is full of inhabitants, and so impracticable to an invader by their numerous stone walls, and a variety of other circumstances, that they need not apprehend danger from attack. They can enjoy their independence without our assistance. If our government is to be founded on equal compact, what inducement can they possibly have to be united with us, if we do not grant them some privileges with regard to their shipping? Suppose they were to unite with us without having those privileges, can we flatter ourselves that such union would be lasting? Interest and policy concurred in prevailing upon us to submit the regulation of commerce to the General Government. But justice and humanity require it likewise. Who have been the greatest sufferers in the Union by our obtaining our independence? The Eastern States. They have lost everything but their country and freedom. As to the restriction upon the African trade after 1808, your delegates had to contend with the religious and political prejudices of the Eastern and Middle States, and the interested and inconsistent opinion of Virginia. So long as there is an acre of swamp-land uncultivated in South

Carolina, I favor the importation of negroes. Our climate, and the flat, swampy situation of our country, oblige us to cultivate our lands with them. Without them the State would be a desert. Those members of the Convention who opposed an unlimited importation, alleged that slaves increased the weakness of any State which admitted them; that they were a dangerous species of property, which an invading enemy could easily turn against ourselves and the neighboring States, and that as we were allowed a representation for them, our influence in the government would be increased in proportion, as we were less able to defend ourselves. Show us some period, said the members from the Eastern States, when it may be in our power, if we please, to put a stop to the importation of this weakness, and we will endeavor, for your convenience, to restrain the religious and political prejudices of our people upon this subject. The Middle States and Virginia made no such proposition; they were for immediate and total prohibition. A committee of the States was appointed to accommodate this matter, and, after a great deal of difficulty, it was settled on the footing recited in the Constitution. By this settlement we have secured an unlimited transportation of negroes for twenty years. Nor is it declared that it shall then stop; it may be continued. We have a security that the General Government can never emancipate them, for no such authority is granted, and it is admitted on all hands that the General Government has no powers but what are expressly granted by the Constitution, and that all rights not expressed were reserved by the several States. We have obtained a right to recover our slaves in whatever part of America they may take refuge, which is a right we had not before. We have made the best terms for the security of that species of property it was in our power to make, and upon the whole they are not bad." Mr. Lowndes persisted: "The Confederation recognized the status of the States as fixed by themselves, in the treaty of peace with Great Britain. That recognition did not appear in the proposed plan, and the possibilities of danger from that omission overbalanced any advantages."

Mr. Barnwell characterized the supposed inevitable antagonism of the Eastern States as a prejudice: "There were no facts to support it. When the arm of oppression lay heavy upon us, were they not the first to arouse; when the sword of civil discord was drawn, were they not the first in the field; when war deluged their plains with blood, did they demand Southern troops for the defense of the North; when war floated to the South, did they withhold their assistance? When we stood with the spirit, but the weakness of youth, they supported us with the vigor and prudence of age. When our country was subdued, when our citizens submitted to superior power, those States showed their attachment. I see here no man who does not know that the shackles of the South were broken asunder by the arms of the North. We are indeed in a minority, but there must be a majority somewhere. Either North or South must be in that relation to each other. That this Constitution is not the best possible to be framed is undeniable, but it is the best our situation admits of." Mr. Edward Rutledge compared the governmental powers in the old and new Constitutions: "They differed very little, except in the essential point of giving a power to Government of enforcing its obligations. Surely no man could object to that. So far from not preferring the Northern States with a Navigation Act, policy dictated to us to increase their strength by every means in our power. In the day of danger, we should have no resource but in the naval strength of our Northern friends. We must hold our country by courtesy, unless we have a navy, and can never become a great nation till powerful upon the waters."

General Pinckney dated independence from "that declaration which babes should be taught to lisp in their cradles, youth to recite as an indispensable lesson, young men to regard as their compact of freedom, and the old to repeat with ejaculations of gratitude for the blessings it would bestow on their posterity. The separate independence and individual sovereignty of the several States, were never thought of by the patriots who framed it. The several States are not even mentioned by name in any part of it, as if it were intended to impress this maxim on Americans, that our freedom and independence arose from our Union, and that without it, we could be neither free nor independent. Let us consider all attempts to weaken the Union, by maintaining that each State is separately and individually independent, as a species of political heresy; which can never benefit us, but may bring on us the most serious distresses."

Mr. Lowndes was "pained to appear pertinacious, but as his constituents were in favor of the Constitution, and therefore he should not sit in the Convention, he relied upon the indulgence of the House for the performance of his duty to his State, by whose decision he, as a good citizen, must cheerfully abide. The arguments adduced he must consider specious. Supposing we considered ourselves so aggrieved as to insist on redress, what was the probability of relief? In revolving a misfortune, some little gleams of comfort resulted from a hope of being able to resort to an impartial tribunal. Would that be found in Congress? As to migration from the Eastern to the Southern States, our country from its excessive heats is so uncomfortable, that our acquaintance is rather shunned than solicited."

Mr. Lincoln "had listened with eager attention to all the arguments in favor of the Constitution, and the more he heard the more he was convinced of its evil tendency.

You contended ten years for liberty. What is liberty? The power of governing yourself. If you adopt this Constitution, do you have that power? no; you give to it men who live a thousand miles from you. What security have you for a republican form of government, when it depends upon the will and pleasure of a few men, with an army, a navy, and a rich treasury at their back, to alter and change it at their will?"

The motion for a Convention passed by a majority of one. Of the opposition as of the advocacy in that Convention, a solitary memorial is extant.

Patrick Dollard claimed that "his people, the people of Prince Frederick Parish, were brave, honest, and industrious, and that they had been conspicuous in the late bloody struggle. Nearly to a man they are opposed to this Constitution. Willing to vest ample and sufficient powers in Congress, they will not agree to make over to them, or to any set of men, their birthright. They are highly alarmed at the long and rapid strides taken in this Constitution toward despotism. They say it is big with political evils, and pregnant with a great variety of woes to the people of the Southern States, and especially to South Carolina; that it is particularly calculated for a despotic aristocracy, and carries with it the appearance of a phrase much in use in despotic reigns, the favorite of Archbishop Laud—'non-resistance.'"

The Constitution was adopted, by a vote of one hundred and forty-nine to seventy-three.

THE CHARLESTON CONVENTION, 1860.

THE Charleston Convention was as important in its effects as any that ever met in the United States, and, although a party Convention, deserves the same consideration as the Federal and ratifying Conventions; for there the majority of the Democratic party of the free States renounced the principles on which the Jeffersonian party had succeeded in 1800. The southern claim in that Convention was no new claim, an assertion of passion, or a manœuvre of politicians, but the deliberate conviction of every year since the ratification of the Constitution—a ratification mainly due in the Southern States to the slaveholding interest. In 1826, Hayne expressed the sense of rights, in defense of which the non-slaveholder and the slaveholder were ready to risk any extremity:

"The question of slavery is one in all its bearings of extreme delicacy, concerning which I know of but a single wise and safe rule, either for the States in which it exists or for the Union. It must be considered and treated entirely as a domestic question. In respect to foreign nations, the language of the United States ought to be, that it concerns the peace of our political family, and therefore we can not permit it to be touched; and in respect to the slaveholding States, the only safe and constitutional ground on which they can stand is, that they will not permit it to be called in question either by their sister States or by the Federal Government. It is a subject upon which I always advert with exteme reluctance—never, until it is forced upon me. I consider our rights in that species of property as not open even to discussion, either here or elsewhere, and duties imposed by our situation, we are not to be taught by fanatics political or religious. To call into question our rights, is gravely to violate them; to attempt to instruct us on the subject, is to insult us; to assail our institutions, is wantonly to invade our peace. The Southern States will never permit, never can permit, any interference whatever in their domestic concerns, and the very day on which the attempt shall be made by the authorities of the Federal Government we will consider ourselves driven out of the Union!"

On the 23d of April, 1860, the delegates to a National Democratic Convention met at Charleston. Called to order, and a president *pro tem.* appointed, it proceeded to complete its organization. A committee on organization and a committee on credentials were constituted. In each, the delegations selected one of their number to represent them. Contesting delegations from New York and Illinois being present, the Convention ordered neither of the sitting delegations to vote in their own case. An attempt to exclude a contested delegation (until the right was adjudicated) from any action in the Convention, had previously been made, but failed.

The committee on organization reported a list of officers, Caleb Cushing (of Massachusetts) the president. It recommended that the rules and regulations of the Conventions of 1852 and 1856 be adopted, with the addition "That in any State which has not provided, or directed by its State Convention, how the vote may be given, the Convention will recognize the right of each delegate to cast his individual vote."

To the officers reported there was no objection, to the additional rule there was; and, a division of the question being demanded, the first clause only was carried. The retiring president and his successor addressed the Convention. The former urged the fact that the Democratic party knew no sections of the Union, its tie of brotherhood, East, West, North, and South, being a common belief in certain political principles. The latter asserted that the mission of the party had been, and was, to maintain the public liberties, to reconcile popular freedom with order, to maintain the sacred reserved rights of the States, and to stand sentinel at the outposts of the Constitution. He characterized the other party as aiming at a sectional conspiracy of one half of the States against the other half, with the mingled stupidity and insanity of fanaticism, hurrying the land to revolution and civil war. Business resumed, a committee to report a platform and resolutions was constituted, each delegation selecting one of its members to sit. Until a platform should have been adopted, the Convention determined not to ballot for nominees.

The majority report of the committee on credentials (adopted) awarded seats to the sitting delegations and delegates.

The minority report (rejected) divided the vote of New York equally between the contesting delegations.

The committee on the platform, by its chairman, presented a report, the judgment of seventeen States:

"That the platform adopted at Cincinnati be affirmed, with the following resolutions:

"1. The national Democracy of the United States hold these cardinal principles upon the subject of slavery in the Territories: That Congress has no power to abolish slavery in the Territories; that a Territorial Legislature has no power to abolish slavery in the Territories, nor to prohibit the introduction of slaves, nor any power to exclude slavery therefrom, nor any power to destroy or impair the right of property in slaves, by any legislation whatsoever.

"2. That the enactments of State Legislatures to defeat the faithful execution of the fugitive-slave law are hostile in character, subversive of the Constitution, and revolutionary in their effect.

"3. That it is the duty of the Federal Government to protect, when necessary, the rights of persons and property on the high-seas, in the Territories, or wherever else its constitutional authority extends.

"4. That the Democracy of the nation recognizes the imperative duty of the Government to protect the naturalized citizen in all his rights, whether at home or in foreign lands, to the same extent as its native citizens.

"5. The national Democracy earnestly recommends the acquisition of the Island of Cuba at the earliest practicable period.

"6. Whereas, one of the greatest necessities of the age, in a political, commercial, postal, and military point of view, is a speedy communication between the Atlantic and Pacific coasts, therefore, that the national Democratic party hereby pledge themselves to use every means in their power to secure the passage of some bill for the construction of a Pacific Railroad from the Mississippi River to the Pacific Ocean at the earliest practicable moment."

Payne (of Ohio) presented a minority report, which embodied the views of fifteen States:

"We, the Democracy of the Union, in convention assembled, hereby declare our affirmance of the resolutions unanimously adopted and declared as a platform of principles by the Democratic Convention at Cincinnati in the year 1856, believing that Democratic principles are unchangeable in their nature when applied to the same subject-matter, and we recommend as the only further resolutions the following:

"That all questions in regard to rights of property in States or Territories are judicial in their character, and the

Democratic party is pledged to abide by, and faithfully carry out, such determination of those questions as has been, or may be, made by the Supreme Court of the United States.

"That it is the duty of the United States to afford ample and complete protection to all its citizens, whether at home or abroad, whether native or foreign born.

"That one of the necessities of the age, in a military, commercial, and postal point of view, is speedy communication between the Atlantic and the Pacific States, and the Democratic party pledge such constitutional government aid as will insure the construction of a railroad to the Pacific coast at the earliest practicable period.

"That the Democratic party are in favor of the acquisition of the Island of Cuba on such terms as shall be honorable to ourselves and just to Spain.

"That the enactments of State Legislatures to defeat the faithful execution of the fugitive-slave law are hostile in character, subversive of the Constitution, and revolutionary in effect."

Butler (of Massachusetts) presented a second minority platform:

"We, the Democracy of the Union, in convention assembled, hereby declare our affirmance of the Democratic resolutions unanimously adopted and declared as a platform of principles at Cincinnati, in the year 1856, without addition or alteration, believing that Democratic principles are unchangeable in their nature when applied to the same subject-matter, and we recommend as the only further resolution the following:

"It is the duty of the United States to extend its protection alike over all its citizens, whether native or naturalized."

Cochrane (of New York) offered an amendment to the Butler report:

"That the several States of the Union are, under the Constitution, equal, and that the people thereof are entitled to the free and undisturbed possession of their rights of person and property in the common Territories; and that any attempt by Congress or a Territorial Legislature to annul, abridge, or discriminate against such equality or rights would be unwise in policy and repugnant to the Constitution; and that it is the duty of the Federal Government, whenever such rights are violated, to afford the necessary, proper, and constitutional remedies for such violations; that the platform of principles adopted by the Convention at Cincinnati, and the foregoing resolutions, are hereby declared the platform of the Democratic party."

The proposition of Mr. Cochrane, being a third amendment, could not, under the rules, be considered, and Bigler (of Pennsylvania) moved that the majority and minority reports be recommitted to the committee, with instructions to report in an hour the following resolutions:

"That the platform adopted by the Democratic party at Charleston be affirmed, with the following explanatory resolutions:

"That the government of a Territory organized by an act of Congress is provisional and temporary, and during its existence all citizens of the United States have an equal right to settle in the Territory, without their rights either of person or property being destroyed or impaired by Congressional or Territorial legislation.

"That it is the duty of the United States to maintain all the constitutional rights of property in the Territories, and to enforce all decisions of the Supreme Court in reference thereto," etc.*

A division of the question being demanded, recommitment was ordered, but the instructions were tabled.

---

* Those resolutions on which there was substantial agreement will be designated by "etc."

At this stage the rule of the Convention as to the unit and individual vote had to be construed. Georgia "requested" its delegates to vote as a unit. The chair decided that so its vote must be cast. Later, New Jersey having instructed its delegation to vote on one subject as a unit, and "recommended" it to vote as a unit upon all other subjects, the chair decided that its vote must be cast as a unit. The decision, on appeal, was overruled.

The committee on the platform and resolutions reported (its chairman stating that its report was understood to embody in substance the views of Bayard, Cochrane, and Bigler):

"That the platform adopted by the Democratic party at Cincinnati be affirmed, with the following explanatory resolutions:

"That the government of a Territory organized by an act of Congress is provisional and temporary, and during its existence all citizens of the United States have an equal right to settle with their property in the Territory, without their rights either of person or property being destroyed or impaired by Congressional or Territorial legislation. That it is the duty of the Federal Government, in all its departments, to protect, when necessary, the rights of persons and property in the Territories or wherever its constitutional authority extends.

"That when the settlers in a Territory have an adequate population, and form a State Constitution, the right of sovereignty commences, and, being consummated by admission into the Union, they stand on an equal footing with the people of the other States; and the State thus organized ought to be admitted into the Federal Union, whether its Constitution prohibits or recognizes the institution of slavery," etc.

The minority submitted its report:

"That we, the Democracy of the Union, in convention

assembled, hereby declare our affirmance of the resolutions unanimously adopted and declared as a platform of principles by the Democratic Convention at Cincinnati in the year 1856, believing that Democratic principles are unchangeable in their nature when applied to the same subject-matter, and we recommend as the only further resolutions the following:

"Inasmuch as difference of opinion exists in the Democratic party, as to the nature and extent of the powers of a Territorial Legislature, and as to the powers and duties of Congress, under the Constitution of the United States, over the institution of slavery within the Territories:

"*Resolved*, that the Democratic party will abide by the decisions of the Supreme Court of the United States upon those questions of constitutional law," etc.

The second minority report (Butler) repeated the original words.

The question was first taken upon the Butler report. It was rejected. The minority report was then adopted as a substitute for the majority report. A division of the question being demanded, separate votes were taken upon each of its propositions: that which pledged the Democratic party to abide by the decisions of the Supreme Court upon questions of the nature and extent of the powers of a Territorial Legislature, and of the powers and duties of Congress in regard to slavery in the Territories, was defeated; the others were adopted.

Stuart (of Michigan) moved to reconsider, and also to lay the motion to reconsider upon the table, but gave way to Walker (of Alabama), who, under instructions from his delegation, presented a communication to the chair, and announced that Alabama withdrew from the Convention. The delegations from Mississippi, South Carolina, Florida, Texas, Louisiana, and Arkansas followed the same course, and duly announced the same. As the reasoning in each communication was identical, if its expression varied, the citation of one will exhibit all.

"*To the President of the Democratic Convention.*

"SIR: As chairman of the delegation which has the honor to represent Mississippi on this floor, I desire to be heard by you, and by the Convention.

"In common consultation we have met here, the representatives of sister States, to resolve the principles of a great party. While maintaining principles, we profess no spirit save that of harmony, conciliation, the success of our party, and the safety of our organization. But to the former the latter must yield, for no organization is valuable without it, and no success is honorable which does not crown it.

"We came here simply asking a recognition of the equal rights of our State under the laws and Constitution of our common Government, that our rights of property should be asserted, and the protection of that property, when necessary, should be yielded by the Government which claims our allegiance. We had regarded government and protection as correlative ideas, and, so long as the one was maintained, the other still endured. After a deliberation of many days it has been announced to us by a controlling majority of nearly one half of the States of the Union, and that, too, in the most solemn and impressive manner, that our demand can not be met, and our rights can not be recognized. While it is granted that the capacity of the Federal Government is ample to protect all other property within its jurisdiction, it is claimed to be impotent when called upon to act in favor of a species of property recognized in fifteen sovereign States. Within those States, even Black Republicans admit it to be guaranteed by the Constitution, and to be only assailed by a higher law; without, they claim the right to prohibit and destroy it. The controlling majority of Northern representatives on this floor, while they deny all power to destroy, equally deny all power to protect; and this, they assure us, is, and must, and shall be the condition of our co-operation in the next presidential election.

"In this state of affairs our duty is plain and obvious. The State which sent us here announced to us her principles. In common with seventeen of her sister States, she has asked a recognition of her constitutional rights. They have been plainly and explicitly denied to her. We have offered to yield everything, except an abandonment of her rights; everything, except her honor, and it has availed us nothing.

"As representatives of Mississippi, knowing her wishes, as honorable men, regarding her commands, we withdraw from the Convention, and, so far as our action is concerned, absolve her from all connection with this body, and all responsibility for its action.

"To you, sir, as presiding officer of the Convention, while it has existed in its integrity, we desire, collectively, as a delegation, and individually, as men, to tender the highest assurances of our profound respect and consideration."

The communication of the Arkansas delegation discloses its additional reason for withdrawal:

"That, by the usages and customs of the Democracy, as developed in its practice in former conventions; by the compact believed to have been made by Democrats of the United States, when conventions were first agreed to be founded; the report of the committee on the platform became the platform of the party, and therefore this Convention had no duty to perform in relation thereto, but to receive, confirm, and publish the same, and cause it to be carried into effect, wherever in the respective States the Democracy were able to enforce their decrees at the ballot-box.

"This opinion is confirmed by the history of the past, which shows that in all instances the sovereignty of the States, not the electoral vote of the States, has uniformly been represented in the committee on a platform, and that the report of the committee has invariably been registered as the supreme law of the Democratic party, by unanimous consent of the entire Convention, without changing or in any manner altering any part or portion thereof. It is a part of our traditional learning, confidently believed, that the Democracy of the United States, by a peculiar system of checks and balances, formed after the fashion of the Federal Government, had contracted and bound themselves to fully recognize the sovereignty of the States in making the platform, and of the population or masses of the States in naming the candidate to be placed on the platform. That many States have been uniformly allowed to vote the full strength of their electoral college in these conventions, when it was well known that the said States had never heretofore, and probably would never hereafter, give a single electoral vote at the polls to the candidate whom they had so large a share in nominating, can not be accounted for on any other principle than that it was intended as a recognition of the sovereignty and equality of said States.

"Would it be right for the numerical majority to deprive the Black Republican States, represented on this floor, of the representation which by custom they have so long enjoyed, because it is evident that they will be unable to vote the Democratic ticket in the next presidential election? If wrong, how much more unjust to deprive all the States of their vested right to make and declare the platform in the usual and customary manner! The South has heretofore felt safe, because of the checks and balances imposed upon the machinery of conventions. Where she retained an equal power to write the creed of faith, she could trust her Northern sisters, with their immense populations, to name the candidate, and all would alike support the creed and the candidate."

Twenty-six of the thirty-six delegates from Georgia announced that they withdrew from the Convention. Ten refused to abide by their decision, but when they sought to vote, the vote was challenged, and the chair decided that, under the instructions of Georgia to its delegation, they were excluded from separate action. Upon an appeal, the Convention sustained the chair.

It is clear now, if it was not then, that upon the nature of a federal republic, upon the scope of a Constitution, and upon the principles of the Democratic party, there was a divergence between the Democracy North and South, too radical to admit of further concert of action. Between the Republican party and the Northern Democracy the distinction was of form, not substance.* Both claimed that a numerical majority could rightfully dictate to the Southern States what thenceforth should be their constitutional rights; one, through the agency of elections, the other, through that of party conventions. The "bad robber" in the nursery tale proposes to dispatch "the babes in the wood" at a blow. The "good robber" prevents by killing him, and then leaves the children to die from starvation. The Southern claim of rights had only the choice between the "bad robber" and the "good robber."

Mr. Cook (of Ohio) moved that the Convention, by a call of States, proceed to nominate candidates for the presidency and vice-presidency, and asked the previous question, which he withdrew for the moment, whereupon Bidwell (of California) read the resolutions of California:

* The Democratic party in the free States was far from unanimity; at least one third held to its once universal theory of constitutional rights, but of course was powerless.

"1. That the platform adopted at Cincinnati, in 1856, is hereby affirmed.

"2. That to entitle a Territory to form a Constitution for admission into the Union as a sovereign State, it should contain a reasonable number of inhabitants, not less than the number required for a representative in Congress.

"3. That the true interpretation of the Cincinnati platform is hereby declared to be, that the right to hold slaves in a Territory rests on the same ground and is entitled to the same protection as other property.

"4. That any infraction of the rights of property in a Territory would be a judicial question, and that it is the duty of Congress to pass such laws as may be necessary to secure the faithful execution of the mandates of the courts.

"5. That Congress has the power at any time to change or repeal any Territoral organic act, and to revise or annul any Territorial act conflicting therewith."

Howard (of Tennessee) offered a resolution, "That the president of the Convention be directed not to declare any person nominated for the office of President or Vice-President, who has not received a number of votes equal to two thirds of the votes of all the electoral colleges." Mr. Cook called up his resolution, upon which the previous question had already been moved and seconded. It was carried.

Against the Howard resolution a point of order was made, that in effect it changed an existing rule of the Convention, viz., "That two thirds of the votes given shall nominate," and must therefore lie over a day. The chair decided that the resolution was in order. Upon an appeal, the decision was sustained, and then the resolution was carried.

Douglas, Guthrie, Dickinson, Hunter, Johnson, Lane, were then nominated by delegations or delegates. Fifty-seven ballots were taken without a result. The vote for Douglas was constant at 150 to 152, for the other candidates

100 to 102. Having become satisfied that a nomination was impossible either with or without the Howard resolution, the Convention adjourned, to reassemble at Baltimore on the 18th of June. It recommended to the Democratic party of the several States the filling of all vacancies in their respective delegations.

The clause in the Constitution, upon the meaning of which the free and the slave States crossed swords, is:

"The Congress shall have power to dispose of, and make all needful rules and regulations respecting the Territory, or other property belonging to the United States; and nothing in this Constitution shall be construed to prejudice any claim of the United States, or of any particular State."

In the Federal Convention that clause was accepted instantly and almost unanimously.* In the ratifying conventions of the States, while almost every other delegation of power was subjected to sharp scrutiny, acute criticism, and demand for exposition, that was admitted without question, though even the jurisdiction over ten miles square excited jealousy. It is evident that all men then understood it alike, or supposed that they did.

---

* Maryland only, No.

THE CHARLESTON CONVENTION ADJOURNED TO BALTIMORE.

To appreciate easily the proceedings of the Convention at Baltimore, the situation must be understood.

The Federal Government, under its power to dispose of the Territory, etc., causes the land to be surveyed and divided into plots. It establishes land-offices to sell and to give evidences of title under its laws. It commissions a Governor, and, under its authority, a Territorial Legislature is elected. When satisfied that the population is sufficient, it authorizes, or recognizes, a Convention called to frame a Constitution. Upon that Constitution it admits the Territory into the Union, as a State. No one, therefore, denied that the Convention which framed a Constitution could settle therein its internal policy as to property in slaves. Before it became a State, the status of that property in it was the bone of contention. The Republican party held that the words "to make all necessary rules and regulations for the disposal," invested the Federal Government with the right to prohibit slavery in the Territories. This position the Democratic party denied, but, as to the power of a Territorial Legislature on the subject, Democrats in different sections of the Union differed widely. A majority of them in the Free States held that the right of property in slaves was a subject within the jurisdiction of a Territorial Legislature, and that its action thereon was beyond the jurisdiction of the Federal authority. This doctrine was known as "non-intervention" and "popular sovereignty."

A minority of them in the free States, and nearly all in the slave States, held that non-intervention was practically hostile intervention, because property of every kind, only existing by convention, and only continuing to exist by the protection of law, the abdication by the Federal Government of the duty of protecting any species of property in the Territories was equivalent to destroying it; that non-intervention vested in a Territorial Legislature of a few thousand settlers a power not possessed by the Federal Government, and therefore not communicable by it; a power only capable of being exercised by three fourths of the States; and that it assumed, in addition, a question to be open, which was closed by the Constitution. Common right in each State for a citizen of it to enter into a Territory with such property as his State recognized, and to keep it, protected by the Union, until the Territory was admitted as a State, had been denied by a majority at Charleston, which equally denied the right of an appeal to and of a decision by the constitutional umpire, the Supreme Court, the practical effect being to make the will of a majority, the Constitution. Hence the secession of delegations.

Mr. Douglas, a man of remarkable energy and ability, was so committed to "non-intervention at all hazards," that he could not, with a decent regard to consistency, accept a nomination upon any platform which did not recognize, still less upon one which conflicted with it. His following could have nominated him at Charleston after the secessions, by rescinding the two-thirds rule, but, as neither the platform nor the nomination in that case could have received the vote of a single Southern State, he would have been a sectional candidate upon a sectional platform; therefore the Convention was adjourned to Baltimore, in the hope that some, if not all of the Southern States would sacrifice constitutional belief for the unity of the party.

At the assemblage of the Convention, the president directed those States present at the adjournment to be called. They being reported by the secretary present, he called the body to order, and stated the business left unfinished—the resolutions constituting a platform, and the ulterior question of adopting the majority report as amended. He recalled the fact that a motion to proceed to a ballot for nominations had been carried, under which many ballotings had been taken; then, that motion had been laid on the table, and a motion to adjourn had been carried, with a recommendation to the several States to supply vacancies in their delegations, the construction of which language, and the scope of its application, the Convention, not the chair, must determine. The chair had received communications purporting to be the credentials of delegations from certain States; they would be submitted to the Convention, the chair having no authority to canvass credentials. The president then briefly urged the necessity of maintaining the integrity of the Democratic party, as the issue, in the political contest about to be waged, was victory or defeat for the Constitution.

The first question to be settled was the meaning of vacancies. The chair decided that it had neither the power to decide whether there were or were not vacancies, nor the right to make a suggestion to the Convention on the subject. The question was settled by the adoption of a resolution offered by Mr. Church (of New York), "That the credentials of all persons claiming seats in this Convention, made vacant by the secession of delegates at Charleston, be referred to the committee on credentials, and said committee is instructed, as soon as practicable, to examine and report the names of persons entitled to such seats." By unanimous consent, the claims of contesting delegates to seats in the sitting delegations were referred to the same committee.

The majority of the committee reported that the seats of the original delegations from Alabama, Mississippi, Louisiana, Texas, and Florida had become vacant; that those from Georgia, Arkansas, and Delaware had become partially so; that from Florida none appeared with credentials; that from Mississippi and Texas there were delegations whose claim to seats was not contested; that there were two delegations from Arkansas, one of three, one of six, claiming the three vacant seats, which should be admitted, the six to cast two of the votes, the three, one; but if either should neglect to take their seats or cast their votes, the other should cast the three votes.

That the delegation from Louisiana (the Soulé) be admitted.

That the delegation from Alabama (the Forsyth) be admitted.

That the delegation from Texas be admitted.

That the delegation from Georgia, of which H. L. Beming is chairman, be admitted, with power to cast half the vote of the State; that the delegation of which Colonel Gardner is chairman be admitted, with power to cast half the vote of the State; and if either of the delegations neglected or refused to cast the vote as above indicated, that the ten delegates present may cast the whole vote of the State; that James A. Bayard and William G. Whitely are entitled to seats from the county of New Castle, Delaware.

That R. L. Chaffee, who (as substitute for B. F. Hallett) was admitted at Charleston, is entitled to a seat, and said Hallett, who has assumed said seat, is not.

That John O. Fallon, Jr. (as substitute for Gardy), duly admitted at Charleston as a delegate from the Eighth Congressional District of Missouri, is entitled to a seat.

A minority report gave seats to Hallett, of Massachusetts; to Gardy, of Missouri; and to Bayard and Whitely as delegates from Delaware. It held that the original delegations from Alabama, Arkansas, Georgia, Louisiana, and Texas were entitled to seats; as to Mississippi, agreeing with the majority. It advised that the delegation from Florida to Charleston be invited to take seats and cast the vote of Florida. Its reasoning was, that "vacancies in a delegation" meant and was intended to mean vacancies, not new delegations; that the original delegations continued such until the power which had conferred withdrew their function; but if otherwise, a new delegation must be commissioned by the same authority which had commissioned the old. "The right of persons to seats is to be determined by the fact that they were appointed according to its usages by the constituency they claim to represent; wanting those essential prerequisites, they are not entitled to seats, even if there are no contestants; with them, they are entitled to seats, if there are contestants." The facts which the report stated as the basis of its conclusions are:

In Alabama, Georgia, and Mississippi, the Democratic Executive Committees had called conventions of the party, by which the course of their delegations at Charleston had been approved, and they were accredited to Baltimore. In Louisiana the old Convention was reassembled, a new Convention not being possible; in that, the course of its delegation at Charleston was approved, and it was accredited to Baltimore. In Texas, time not permitting the assemblage of its Democracy in convention, its Executive Committee accredited the delegation to Baltimore. In Delaware, under the rules of the party, the old Convention reassembled and acted.

The majority report, except as to the Georgia delegation, was adopted. Upon the motion of Mr. Church (of

New York), the old delegation was declared entitled to seats. The chair thereupon directed tickets to be issued to the admitted delegates. Russell (of Virginia) then announced, by the instructions of a large majority of the delegation, that they could no longer participate in the deliberations of the Convention, having, in their judgment, exhausted all honorable efforts to avert that necessity, and having arrived at that conclusion after long, mature, and anxious consideration.

Lauder (of North Carolina) had the painful duty imposed on him to announce that a very large majority of the delegation of North Carolina were compelled to retire from the Convention. The recent vote had satisfied them that the Northern Democracy was no longer willing to attribute to the South equality in the Union.

Ewing (of Tennessee) stated that the Tennessee delegation had exhibited, as far as they knew how, an anxious desire to harmonize the Convention, but, upon the result that day obtained, twenty of its members would have to retire. Four would remain.

Stevens (of Oregon): "By the action to-day delegations as much entitled to seats as our own have been excluded. For this injustice to and ignoring of the weaker States, the delegation from Oregon will take no further part in the deliberations of the Convention."

Ten of the delegation from Kentucky deemed it inconsistent with duty to themselves and to their constituents to participate further in the deliberations of the Convention. Five, "without intending to vacate our seats, and with the intention of co-operating with the Convention, if its unity and harmony be restored by any future event, will not in the mean time participate in its deliberations, nor hold ourselves or our constituents bound by its action."

Two delegates from Missouri then retired from the Convention. A vote upon the resolution to proceed to nominate candidates for the presidency and vice-presidency being in order, the chair addressed the Convention:

"The delegations of a majority of the States of this Union have, either in whole or in part, in one form or another, ceased to participate in the deliberations of this body. I deem it due to myself, and to the members of the Convention, as to whom my action would no longer represent the will of a majority of the Convention, to resign my office, take my seat as one of the Massachusetts delegation, and abide its determination upon the future action of the Convention." The admission of sham delegations was the cause of these withdrawals.

David Todd (of Ohio) assumed the chair, and stated that, if there were no privileged questions intervening, the secretary would proceed with the call of the States.

Mr. Butler attempted to address the chair to present a protest, and asked the same respectful hearing for Massachusetts which had been given to everybody else. Objection being made, he was compelled to be silent until Massachusetts was called. He then, under instructions from the majority of the delegation, presented a protest against the action of the Convention in excluding Mr. Hallett. He also announced that part of the Massachusetts delegation would no longer participate in the deliberations of the Convention. The members whom he spoke of thereupon retired.

Two ballotings were had; in the latter one hundred and ninety-four and a half votes were cast, of which one hundred and eighty-one and a half were for Douglas, who was thereupon, by unanimous resolution, declared the regular nominee of the Democratic party. Benjamin Fitzpatrick received the nomination as Vice-President. He declined, and the nomination was then tendered by the National Democratic Committee to Herschel V. Johnson (of Georgia), who accepted.

After the nomination, the Convention, with but one or two dissenting voices, resolved,

"That it is in accordance with the interpretation of the Cincinnati platform that, during the existence of the Territorial governments, the measure of restriction, whatever it may be, imposed by the Federal Constitution on the power of the Territorial Legislature over the subject of the domestic relations, as the same has been, or shall hereafter be, finally determined by the Supreme Court of the United States, should be respected by all good citizens, and enforced with promptness and fidelity by every branch of the General Government."

If this resolution was meant to embody the resolution to the same apparent effect rejected at Charleston, it would seem wiser to have adopted it there, where it might have averted a secession. If its ambiguity in the words "domestic relations" was meant "to keep the promise to the ear and break it to the hope," the attempt at a trap for voters was not successful. It nowhere appears in the record of the Baltimore Convention that the unfinished business, stated by the chair after its organization, was considered; if so, and any action were needed to establish a platform, none existed.

The temper of the free-State delegations can not be misunderstood or misrepresented, for it found expression. "Admit that we are wrong," said Church, "we have the right to be wrong." The right to be wrong may be inseparable from any political relation between communities or individuals, but the English race has always been impatient of the claim.*

---

* After the election of Jefferson, some men, timid from his application of the fourth premise of the Declaration of Independence to the Union, asked him how he construed the Constitution. As its friends asserted it to be, and the people believed, matters of full publicity and general notoriety, was the answer. As contract must be a conception of the mind before honesty

One lesson taught by the history of the Charleston Convention is, that a rule of voting in such a body should be uniform—the individual vote or the vote by delegations. Either is fair, though the former seems more commendable, but no other rule is fair. Another is the necessity, in public as in private affairs, of avoiding the use of terms necessarily ambiguous. The word "people," in the Territorial dispute, was the source of untold woes. Men could and would construe it by their desires. Therefore, if an umpire was rejected, they must quarrel. To the construction of language the majority principle is not applicable. Six men have no more natural right to govern five men than five to govern six. If the eleven agree that upon any subjects the will of six shall control that of five, to such extent the majority has the right of sway, and the minority the duty of obedience. But, if there is a dispute as to what they had agreed on, the right derived from agreement no longer exists. They then stand as before the compact, and must find an umpire, separate, or fight.

---

can be a conception, as a denial of contract must be a rejection of honesty, the Jeffersonian party held the Constitution to be a mutual contract of the States, honesty as indispensable between States in a Union as between men in a society; and the law of contract to be, that a disregard of it by one party is the absolution from it of another party. In communities whose religion is the belief of a covenant made by God with one race, amplified and extended through his Son to all races, the relation which the Omnipotent thought fit between Omnipotence and men, ought to be recognized as just between men and men and States and States. If there be any obligation with a divine sanction, it is that of covenant. Very many of the party in the free States, which asserted itself the heir of the Jeffersonian party, substituted sentimentality, which is self-indulgence, for honesty, which is self-control.

THE END.

HISTORY OF THE PEOPLE OF THE UNITED STATES, from the Revolution to the Civil War. By JOHN BACH McMASTER. To be completed in five volumes. Vols. I and II, 8vo, cloth, gilt top, $2.50 each.

SCOPE OF THE WORK.—*In the course of this narrative much is written of wars, conspiracies, and rebellions; of Presidents, of Congresses, of embassies, of treaties, of the ambition of political leaders, and of the rise of great parties in the nation. Yet the history of the people is the chief theme. At every stage of the splendid progress which separates the America of Washington and Adams from the America in which we live, it has been the author's purpose to describe the dress, the occupations, the amusements, the literary canons of the times; to note the changes of manners and morals; to trace the growth of that humane spirit which abolished punishment for debt, and reformed the discipline of prisons and of jails; to recount the manifold improvements which, in a thousand ways, have multiplied the conveniences of life and ministered to the happiness of our race; to describe the rise and progress of that long series of mechanical inventions and discoveries which is now the admiration of the world, and our just pride and boast; to tell how, under the benign influence of liberty and peace, there sprang up, in the course of a single century, a prosperity unparalleled in the annals of human affairs.*

"The pledge given by Mr. McMaster, that 'the history of the people shall be the chief theme,' is punctiliously and satisfactorily fulfilled. He carries out his promise in a complete, vivid, and delightful way. We should add that the literary execution of the work is worthy of the indefatigable industry and unceasing vigilance with which the stores of historical material have been accumulated, weighed, and sifted. The cardinal qualities of style, lucidity, animation, and energy, are everywhere present. Seldom, indeed, has a book, in which matter of substantial value has been so happily united to attractiveness of form, been offered by an American author to his fellow-citizens."—*New York Sun.*

"To recount the marvelous progress of the American people, to describe their life, their literature, their occupations, their amusements, is Mr. McMaster's object. His theme is an important one, and we congratulate him on his success. It has rarely been our province to notice a book with so many excellences and so few defects."—*New York Herald.*

"Mr. McMaster at once shows his grasp of the various themes and his special capacity as a historian of the people. His aim is high, but he hits the mark."—*New York Journal of Commerce.*

"I have had to read a good deal of history in my day, but I find so much freshness in the way Professor McMaster has treated his subject that it is quite like a new story."—*Philadelphia Press.*

"Mr. McMaster's success as a writer seems to us distinct and decisive. In the first place he has written a remarkably readable history. His style is clear and vigorous, if not always condensed. He has the faculty of felicitous comparison and contrast in a marked degree. Mr. McMaster has produced one of the most spirited of histories, a book which will be widely read, and the entertaining quality of which is conspicuous beyond that of any work of its kind."—*Boston Gazette.*

New York: D. APPLETON & CO., 1, 3, & 5 Bond Street.

AUNT CHARLOTTE'S STORIES OF AMERICAN HISTORY. By CHARLOTTE M. YONGE and H. HASTINGS WELD, D. D. With numerous Illustrations. 12mo, cloth, gilt side and back, $1.50.

"In this book we find well-told and intensely interesting and instructive stories of American history, which should be familiar to every boy and girl in the land. In forty-nine chapters the well-known and popular authors have embodied the essential facts of American history from the earliest period to the presidency of Chester A. Arthur. It is a book parents and teachers can safely commend to the young; in fact, it would be a gift of usefulness and practical value to any young person."—*Boston Journal of Education.*

ANECDOTES OF THE CIVIL WAR IN THE UNITED STATES. By Brevet Major-General E. D. TOWNSEND, late Adjutant-General U. S. Army. 12mo, cloth, $1.25.

"The work treats in a very pleasant conversational way of various events and incidents, around which our interest lingers, and of which much is here said that has hitherto been unsaid. Among the topics upon which the author dwells, and which may be cited as giving an idea of the scope and nature of his work, are General Scott's loyalty, the defense of Washington, the neutrality of Kentucky, Early's invasion, service in the Adjutant-General's office, President Lincoln's funeral, Fort Sumter, origin of military commissions, Army of the Potomac commanders, etc."—*Washington Daily Post.*

"General Townsend's book is all interesting."—*New York Army and Navy Journal.*

"An agreeable intermingling of personal anecdotes and historical statements. Full of useful information."—*New York Home Journal.*

"The General bore an important and honorable part in the struggle, and has the rare gift of telling briefly, humorously, and pathetically of what he saw and heard during all the eventful years."—*New York Journal of Commerce.*

"The author writes in a charitable spirit of Scott, Stone, Lee, Buckner, Burke, McClellan, Blair, Sheridan, Stanton, Lincoln, and many others. General Townsend fully disposes of the malicious rumor that Stanton committed suicide. These anecdotes are well worth buying and reading from beginning to end."—*New York Christian Advocate.*

FINANCIAL HISTORY OF THE UNITED STATES FROM 1774 TO 1789, embracing the Period of the American Revolution. By ALBERT S. BOLLES. 8vo, cloth, $2.50.

"It fills a place and meets a want which, so far as my observation extends, is not supplied by any one publication."—DAVID A. WELLS.

FINANCIAL HISTORY OF THE UNITED STATES FROM 1789 TO 1860. By ALBERT S. BOLLES. 8vo, cloth, $3.50.

FINANCIAL HISTORY OF THE UNITED STATES FROM 1861 TO 1885. By ALBERT S. BOLLES. 8vo, cloth, $3.50.

New York: D. APPLETON & CO., 1, 3, & 5 Bond Street.

www.ingramcontent.com/pod-product-compliance
Lightning Source LLC
Chambersburg PA
CBHW031112020726
47495CB00007B/2169
9783337418731